An Elephant's Journey

THUNDER

by Erik Daniel Shein
L. M. Reker

Though inspired by true events, this book is a work of fiction. The characters, incidents, and dialogues are products of the author's imagination and are not to be construed as real. Any resemblance to actual events or persons, living or dead, is entirely coincidental.

World Castle Publishing, LLC
Pensacola, Florida
Copyright © 2017 Arkwatch Holdings, LLC, and Erik Daniel Shein
Hardback ISBN: 9781629895635
Paperback ISBN: 9781629895642
eBook ISBN: 9781629895659
LCN: 2016956982
First Edition World Castle Publishing, LLC, March 7, 2017
http://www.worldcastlepublishing.com

Licensing Notes

Requests for information should be addressed to:
Arkwatch Holdings, LLC
4766 East Eden drive
Cave Creek, AZ 85331
Cover: Arkwatch Holdings, LLC and Karen Fuller
Illustrator: Paul Barton, II
Editor: Melissa Davis

A Special Thanks

I would like to thank the following people that believed in our little elephant, Thunder, and the message, making a difference one story at a time: Barbara Nixon, Theresa Gates, Mary Nickum, John Nickum, Darrell Walters, Jimmy Costello, Sherrie Stoops, Julian Gracie, and Alesha and Vera Vanguard.

To the best editors and team in the world, Karen Fuller, and Missy Davis.

Quotes:

The reason I dedicate myself to helping animals so much is because there are already so many people dedicated to hurting them. ~♥~ EDS

"Some people talk to animals. Not many listen though. That's the problem." - #WinnieThePooh

Everybody has a dream, and this is important, but the dreams that come true in your lifetime always find you. EDS

People will never understand the full intelligence of animals if we don't take the time to learn about them…and respect them. :)

Disclaimer:

Heart Haven is secret animal sanctuary consisting of just animals, in book three, Hope Haven is an animal sanctuary for orphaned animals put together by people.

Table of Contents

CHAPTER 1
A NEW LIFE

It was midnight in the forest. The light of the full moon peeked out through the clouds from the horizon, and the smell of the monsoon rain was in the air. Tonight was a special night. Serenity, an African pygmy forest elephant, was going to be a mother for the first time. All the animals in the area had gathered around to witness the birth. The elephant herd formed a protection circle around Serenity, and the male elephant's ears flapped in excitement. The elders of the herd filled the air with low echo sounds to show their approval. It was time!

A new life was always cause for celebration and the animals were all curious by nature.

Monkeys snuck glances from the tree branches above. Frogs hopped closer, their feet suctioned to large elephant ear-shaped leaves that swayed gently in the wind. Even with such a dark night upon them, the animals awaited the newborn calf.

Thunder clapped loud above them, followed by a large streak of light that lit up the sky. The clouds were illuminated in a brilliant flash as they rolled and churned faster with the wind. A steady stream of rain began to fall, and the group of elephants surrounding Serenity tightened their circle to protect her from the heavy flow of water. *Boom!* The sky lit up again as another loud crack of thunder rang out. At that very moment, the baby elephant emerged from the safety of its mother's belly and splashed into the water beneath him. His mother nudged him closer to the edge of the pond.

"That's right." Serenity said gently. "Come out you." She smiled as she helped him stand on solid land.

Suddenly, the elephant herd began to rumble their feet against the soggy ground. Serenity puffed her chest out with pride as the herd, in unison, lifted their trunks to loudly trumpet their jubilation. A few of the males dipped their trunks into the pond to shower the new arrival and his mother. This was a time for celebration. They all had been blessed with a new life.

Serenity wrapped her trunk around the calf's waist to steady him on his feet. "That's it," she said gently. "Almost there." As he stood up, the ground beneath his feet started to tremble and a hush fell over the crowd of animals, before excited murmurs traveled through them. One of the female elephants addressed Serenity, "You should call him Thunder."

"Thunder?" Serenity ran her trunk over his head and her smile grew. "I like it. What do you think, Thunder?"

The baby elephant looked up at his mother adoringly and gave a small trumpet from his trunk and moved his unsteady feet again. When the ground shook again, the herd of elephants cheered. Serenity moved closer to Thunder and he snuggled up against her.

In a few short years, Thunder grew into a fine young elephant, and Serenity was very proud of her son.

In the early morning light, the sun peeked through the clouds. A rainbow brushed its colors against the sky landing into the recess of the Central African Rainforest, where the world was buzzing with life. An African Grey parrot named Penelope soared high above the forest canopy as she surveyed the world around her.

A green tree frog jumped onto a bamboo branch and settled in for a bite. His long tongue zapped an insect from the shoot and gulped it down noisily. When his hungry belly was satisfied, he bounced away onto his next adventure.

The leaves rustled and branches swayed from the squawking birds that were perched at different intervals. Penelope zoomed over them, her wings almost brushing their heads in the process. She disappeared into the trees.

The rainforest was once a wondrous place filled with life forms unimaginable to most. The crushing reality was that life was no longer what it used to be. The lush rainforest, once a thriving, peaceful kingdom of creatures, great and small, has shrunk in size as civilization has encroached its boundaries. Thousands of species have been lost, and the lungs of our great planet are gasping for air.

Balance between the animals and those that they called Uprights was no more. In the beginning, the land had an agreement with the Uprights, that man and animal would find a way to live in harmony. But the humans got greedy and lost their way. Now, there are only a few places left where the natural world remains pure and where its inhabitants still enjoy the lives they were meant to have.

Today was like any other day. An elephant herd came lumbering out of the thick canopy. Four female adults were followed by four calves that were chatting away to each other about the water hole they had just come from. The grown-ups shook their heads at the playful children and smiled to each other.

The green tree frog jumped over Thunder's head and he turned to look at him. "Did you see that, Mama?"

"Yes, Thunder," answered Serenity. She had not really seen the frog, but Serenity had already answered that exact same question a dozen times on their trek back from the pond. By now, the young elephant really did not need an answer, just an acknowledgement of the curious way his mind worked. The elephants continued to walk as the youngsters bantered back and forth.

They did not see the two silverback gorillas sitting on the hill that overlooked the jungle. Harold and Neville both watched the elephants in awe as the young ones played near the watering hole.

Even the gorillas respected the tall treasures that the elephants were. These pachyderms that now searched for safety and space to roam in a receding landscape were innocent, smart, and joyful creatures. Nature had given them long lives and close bonds—when left alone that is.

Even a curious little calf like Thunder is one of only a few, if not the last, generation of gentle giants who have much to teach the Uprights.

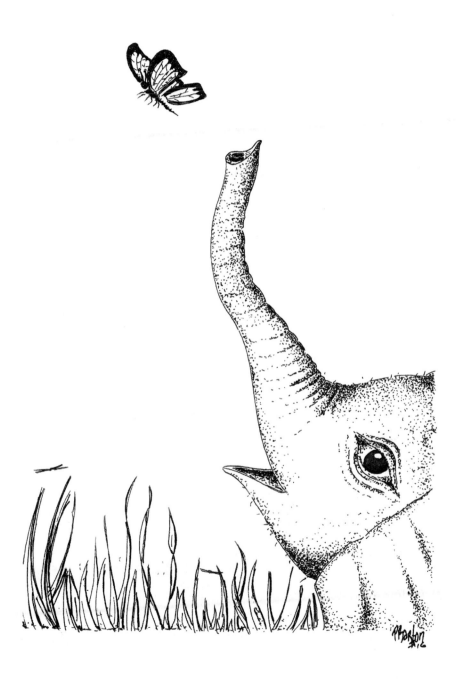

Chapter 2
School is in Session

The pond was filled with sounds of joyful laughter as the elephant calves raced into the water. Playful splashes were followed by deliberate water attacks, as the small tykes shot cold spray from their trunks.

The adults were content to watch the calves play, until the calves turned their attention to their elders. Then all kinds of chaos broke loose as the adults joined in the fun. Soon, it was hard to find where one spray started and the other began. The sounds of trumpeting filled the air, as the elephant herd continued their morning frolic in the water.

When playtime was no more, Thunder followed Serenity out of the water. His legs, once clumsy and loud, were now easily controlled. The ground still trembled when he walked, but he could control the depth of the rumbles by applying different pressures as he moved.

"Aah. Aaahhh. We've arrived." His contented words were easy to understand, having been well washed and entertained. Now he was ready to coat himself, as was his custom after getting fully bathed. He threw small tree limbs over his shoulder with his trunk. A cloud of dust settled over him as he covered himself. Flapping his ears, Thunder giggled uncontrollably.

The first time Thunder had covered himself with mud and dirt after his bath, Serenity had forced him back into the water, but when he had continued to repeat the same process each time, Serenity had learned there were other battles to fight with her offspring. Now, it was simply his pattern.

Serenity smiled at his antics and continued to munch on a branch below her. She casually perused the scene around her. Some elephants were still bathing and drinking from the pond. Others were frolicking in the mud. Their lives were carefree when they were sheltered under the peaceful forest.

A large midnight blue butterfly floated by the scene. Her name was Jennetta Blue and she was attracted to the tiny calf who made the ground tremble like thunder. Flitting closer to him, she passed over his head and floated here and there, until Thunder looked up at her.

Thunder was mesmerized by the beautiful creature. He turned his trunk up to reach her, but she fluttered away before he could make contact. Jennetta Blue disappeared into the trees bordering the watering hole and Thunder stood there, disappointed that the butterfly had not stayed long enough for him to meet her.

Nearby, Serenity called out to the youngsters, "Okay, little ones. Gather around!"

"Coming, Mom." Thunder prodded his large feet onto the ground before him and the dirt shook beneath him. The other calves followed suit, until they were all racing to reach Serenity first.

"This is your next lesson in communication. Everyone in line now."

The young elephants bumped into each other, each one

clamoring to be the first in line. One calf pulled another's tail. Another nudged Thunder out of the way with a little too much zeal, but he returned the favor by stomping his feet, which made the calf move away from his spot. The calves could be competitive from time to time. Their clumsy movements continued to make quite a stir until they finally managed to gather themselves together in a passable line side by side in front of Serenity.

Thoroughly amused, Serenity shook her head and tried to hide her smile at the young ones before continuing. "Wait here."

The elephant moved away from her students and made sure they were paying attention to her before she continued. She emitted a low rumble with her feet. "Okay, kids, can you feel the earth move?"

The young elephants leaned forward on their tiptoes, straining to listen for a sound none of them could hear. Serenity repeated her rumble and Thunder's ears perked up. "I can! I can!"

The calf next to Thunder sneezed absently. He had not heard a thing. His ears flapped slowly in the breeze, and his attention began to waver.

The one to his right stomped the ground in excitement. "I can feel a herd coming."

A male calf further down the line giggled when Serenity rumbled again. "It tickles!"

Serenity smiled at her students. "This is how we send messages. We're the only ones who can do this. When you rumble, other elephants can hear you. The ground vibrates. Like this."

Serenity rumbled again and waited to see how the calves responded. They were starting to get it. "You must listen with your feet."

One of the female calves responded to Serenity in excitement. "I felt it! I felt it! You said, hello!"

Serenity nodded at the calf. "Right! So, let's tell the other herd where we are!"

The calves rumbled together in a soft chorus. The ground began to hum in a gentle vibration. They continued to move until a louder rumble moved through the Earth. In the pond near them, the lily plants began to shake on the surface. Tiny ripples formed in rings around a lily pad, where a green tree frog was resting. He grabbed the closest leaf next to him and slid it over his head to hide under it like a blanket. He let one of his eyes peek out from under the green hideaway as he surveyed his surroundings. When he could not detect the source of the tiny waves in the water, he kept his feet planted firmly on the lily pad beneath him and continued to hide in its camouflaged safety.

Thunder was excited to try it out too. He thought about what he would say for a moment. Then Thunder stomped his feet exuberantly to send his message. He waited anxiously to see if Serenity would understand his communications.

"Bravo, Students! Bravo! Easy, Thunder. They'll hear you just fine without stomping so loud." Serenity smiled at her son.

Thunder bowed his head and a small blush filled his cheeks. "Sorry, Mom."

Serenity's ears perked up. She leaned forward and shuffled her feet slowly. Her feet began to vibrate gently and she looked up to the calves. "They're coming!"

The calves stopped what they were doing and looked up. They trumpeted loudly into the air and waited to greet the herd that was traveling toward them. Five female elephants from another clan trotted out from the rainforest. The children erupted into delightful squeals, as their lesson had brought new friends for them to meet. Another small herd of male elephants joined them. In the next moment the view of the forest was filled with elephants who were entwining their trunks together as they rubbed gently against one another.

Serenity called to Thunder, "C'mon, Thunder. Let's go greet the guests!"

Thunder was about to respond to his mom's request, but Jennetta Blue fluttered near his face. She hovered briefly before him. Thunder smiled at the tiny butterfly. "Hello? What's your name?"

His questions went unanswered for Jennetta Blue flitted away from him toward the forest cove. Thunder's curiosity took over and he moved swiftly after his silent friend.

Serenity called for him, "Thunder!"

Thunder grumbled under his breath. He turned away from his chase and answered, "I'll be right there, Mom."

Two female elephants ran over to Serenity. They each trumpeted their greeting. Their heads rose and their large velvet ears flapped gently. Serenity accepted the embracing trunks that were offered to her. She was happy to see them, and they shared her sentiment. She turned her eyes back to where her calf was trying to chase after a mischievous butterfly. "Thunder! Don't go far!"

Thunder continued his search for Jennetta Blue. He turned to answer his mother, "Okay, Mom."

Thunder entered the forest and came face-to-face with a giant elephant ear plant. His eyes grew wide as he examined the large plant. "Wow! I wonder if my ears will be this big one day." He giggled to himself as he thought about how large his ears would be. "That would be something!" When he ran his trunk over the smooth leaf, he remembered the butterfly and raised head and looked around.

Meanwhile, Jennetta Blue had now completely disappeared from his sight. "Okay, where are you, little butterfly? I know you're here somewhere." Thunder continued to search, hoping to find her. The rest of his day was spent tracking down the midnight blue friend who had playfully evaded him in a game of hide-n-seek that never seemed to get old.

CHAPTER 3
DANGER

A dust cloud chased the truck down a small dirt road away from the rainforest. Drago, an African male in his thirties, sat behind the wheel of his shiny, new pickup. Everything about the vehicle was over the top. The cab was supersized and the truck bed could carry far more than any man really needed. Loud rap music thumped inside the cab of the truck with the bass so loud the windows rattled as he drove down the deserted road.

Turning off the radio, Drago pulled the truck to the side of the road and let it idle quietly in park and got out of the truck. As he gazed at the horizon, his eyes caught something that filled him with delight. He grabbed the binoculars from the small console next to him, and walked to the front of the truck. Putting them up to his eyes, he zoomed in on his quarry. Smiling in satisfaction, he was filled with glee, for now all he saw were dollar signs. What he saw was going to make him so rich! He looked around him, making sure no one else was in sight. It wouldn't do if someone were around to spoil his fun. When he looked back through the lenses, he saw the small elephant herd standing at a watering hole near the edge of the rainforest. He threw the binoculars back inside the truck, then rubbed his hands together in anticipation. An evil grin spread from ear to ear. This was it! That ivory would make him a fortune. Pay day!

Leaping back into the cab, he quickly jammed the gears into drive and made a loud squealing U-turn on the road. Dirt spit from under the tires as they gained traction. Drago stomped his foot on the gas and sped back to the village.

Drago made good time back. Pulling off from the road, he found a parking spot next to the stalls of a rundown outdoor marketplace. He quickly shut off his engine and exited the truck. After locking the doors, he twirled the keys around his finger before shoving them into his pocket. He stopped and made sure he was alone before he smiled, then ducked into the derelict building. He knew his luck was about to change with the information he was about to provide the inhabitants inside.

Seconds later, he emerged from his meeting with an envelope filled so full of cash that crisp hundred dollar bills were sticking out of it. He counted the cash as he unlocked his truck. "Easy pickings," he said to himself and giggled as he counted the money again. He could do this every day, he thought as he settled into the seat.

Drago backed out of his spot, and his truck zipped down the road. Dirt clouded the area around the truck, and a skeleton trinket made of ivory tusk swayed from the rearview mirror. It did not matter what havoc was wreaked. Drago was in it for the money. Always had been and always would be. The only world he believed in was the one that had the most pay day for him. Greed continued to swirl inside his head as he imagined all the things he would buy from this pay load.

Later that day, young elephants played carelessly in their pond. They had no idea that the upright had even seen them. They were innocent to evils of the world; as children are want to be. The calves ran around each other gleefully.

"Let's play Marco Polo," suggested Thunder. His tail swished through the air in excitement.

His friend Destiny replied, "Okay, Thunder. You be Marco first."

"Sure!" Thunder said, then covered his eyes with his ears and counted aloud. "1-2-3-4-5-6-7-8-9-10!"

The other young calves moved around Thunder quietly, which was a feat in itself with their large feet prodding the ground. Thunder kept his eyes closed and called out, "Marco!"

The other calves all responded in unison, "Polo!"

Thunder moved several steps to his right and stopped. His trunk probed the air around him as he tried to feel for one of his friends. When he only felt air, he tried again. "Marco!"

Again his friends replied, "Polo!"

Thunder took a few steps to the right and felt again. "Marco!"

When no one answered, he scratched his head with his trunk. "Hello?" Thunder stood still and leaned forward on his front feet. He heard a calf giggle as the other snuck away from him.

"Marco?" His voice was filled with confusion.

All the calves responded this time. "Polo!"

So far what he was doing was not working, they sounded like they were everywhere at once, so he decided to try a different tactic. Thunder stomped his feet on the ground until it vibrated near him. He moved a little and repeated the process. When he felt a resistance to the vibrations, he knew he was on to something. "Someone must be near."

He was about to tap Destiny when Serenity approached and interrupted their game. "Okay, kids. We have to get going."

A chorus of disgruntled comments was heard next.

Thunder uncovered his eyes and looked up at his mother. "But we just got here."

Destiny soon followed his complaint with her own. "Yeah!"

"Not again!" A few other calves added.

Serenity shook her head softly at them. "I know, but it's not safe. We have to keep moving." She kept her eyes trained to somewhere off in the distance, but none of the calves seemed to notice. Their carefree antics were all they knew of this world.

Thunder stomped his feet in frustration. He did not want to leave the pond. He was quite fond of it, with it being the one place he had spent the majority of his life so far. "I don't wanna go! It's nice here!"

Serenity put her trunk on his head and attempted to comfort her child. "Yes, but things are different now. Home is not a place anymore. Home is who you're with. And we're together. That's the important thing." She ushered them away from the pond.

Thunder and the other calves dropped their heads and trunks in resigned disappointment. They slowly moved on with the herd away from the watering hole and back into the safety of the forest.

A convoy of trucks and Jeeps filled the dirt road leading to where Drago had spotted the herd of elephants. Drago and the other men sported guns and machetes. The men laughed as they drank beer celebrating the news of the elephant herd and its infinite money rewards. They tossed their cans out the windows of their vehicles, mindless to the litter they were creating.

Drago sat in his seat with a smug look of satisfaction on his face. He spoke into the cell phone he held to his ear. "There's a bunch in there. Rhinos, too! Up ahead. Another mile." He laughed into the receiver. "My thoughts exactly! We're going to make a fortune out here. Easy pickings! Mark my words."

The trail of vehicles continued down the road as they searched for their next pay load with no care about the destruction they were about to create. At Drago's command they pulled the vehicles in the nearby field and sat back to wait for sunset.

Inside the forest, birds chirped. Their colors were splendorous against the green leaves. Colobus monkeys swung in the vines above Thunder, and he stopped to stare at them. He noticed the funny monkeys had small faces covered in a velvet gray fur. The outside of their faces were lined with a tuft of white fur that formed a perfect circle. The rest of their bodies were covered with a thick black fur, except for the long fringe of white hair that seemed to line the frame of their backs. Thunder found them quite beautiful and strange because unlike other monkeys he had seen before, these monkeys had no thumbs.

One of the monkeys looked down at him and gave him a warning stare. Apparently, Thunder had glanced upon him a little too long, as the Colobus monkey began to pelt his discarded fruit droppings down at him.

Thunder stepped away from the projectile food, and shook his head in disgust. "Hey! Stop that!"

The monkey squealed at him and shook his head back and forth. Thunder wondered if one of the monkeys might have seen Jennetta Blue. He had seen her moments before, but she had disappeared again. "Do you know where the butterfly went? My mom says they're like angels from heaven."

The monkey nearest him peered down at him. His name was Wallace. "Heaven?"

The second monkey, Willa, jabbed at Wallace playfully. "Heaven's up here in the trees, man. Didn't you know?"

All of the monkeys laughed and one of them slapped his knees playfully. Thunder snorted gently from his trunk. "Very funny."

The third monkey, Weebly, chucked another piece of fruit at Thunder absently before speaking. "Can you fly?" Then the monkeys roared with laughter.

Thunder found his question less than amusing. Elephants fly? "No!"

Weebly tilted his furry face at him. "Can you climb?"

No one waited for his reply. The mere idea of an elephant even attempting to climb up into the trees was hysterical. The monkeys broke out into shrill laughter again. Willa almost lost her perch on the branch she was laughing so hard.

Thunder squeezed the end of his trunk and blew at them.

"Hmph!" Clearly these monkeys would be of no help to him. He stomped his feet and marched away from them, grumbling about their silliness every step.

Willa called out to him. "Oh, don't go away mad! We're just playin'!" The three monkeys all swung closer to Thunder. As he moved, so did they, swinging and jumping from branch to branch.

"Life is full of surprises!" Wallace said cheekily.

Weebly added, "Here comes another one!"

Thunder stomped his feet harder. "Go away!"

Thunder continued on his path that was further away from his mother. He had stayed at a distance as requested until Serenity could feel out the threat level around them. She had been uneasy all afternoon.

Far from Thunder, Serenity was now on guard with their herd. Serenity turned from the group and peered out at the rainforest canopy. She shuffled her feet on the ground and signaled to Thunder. A low rumble emitted from her efforts.

Thunder felt Serenity's low rumble through the ground of the rainforest. He straightened up and raised his ears to pay attention. He knew his mother was not far from him. He looked up at the monkeys that were continuing to pester him. "I better go. I...my mom is calling."

The monkeys gave quick glances to each other. They looked up, down, to the left and the right, and then back at each other again clearly stumped. Wallace scratched his head with his finger before asking the others, "Calling? Did you hear anyone calling?"

Willa replied, "No, did you?"

Wallace let out an annoyed breath before answering. "No."

Weebly added his own reply. "No, me neither."

Willa shook her head and lifted a finger to her head. She made tiny circles in the air. "I think he's gone 'round the block!"

Weebly put a hand to his stomach, rocked back and forth on the tree branch, and giggled in delight. "And then some!"

Wallace looked down at Thunder with a little concern. "Kid, I don't know what you're hearing. Are you hearing voices? Have you had a mental health check-up lately?"

The monkeys broke out in hearty laughter. This time Weebly laughed so hard he fell off the branch then tumbled down toward the floor of the forest.

Willa grabbed him by the tail and swung him back up into the trees before he could hit the ground. Weebly gave her an appreciative glance.

Thunder pounded his front feet and splayed his ears back to listen. He answered them absentmindedly, "No, I haven't! The herd's calling!"

Willa rolled her eyes and shook her head slowly. "Right." She twirled her finger in the air again.

Weebly poked Willa in the stomach before adding, "And Bob's our uncle."

The monkeys howled with laughter. Bob was the turtle that often hung out beneath one of their favorite trees. The idea that monkeys could be related to a turtle was hysterical, but lost on Thunder, who continued to stand and listen for more news from his herd. Thunder stood there patiently, and would stand there for some time hoping that his mother would soon give the all clear for him to come out. That would not be soon enough for his liking.

Just minutes later, Drago and his men pulled all their vehicles to the side. They exited the trucks to start their search for the elephants that Drago had found earlier. Their heavy black boots crushed all plant life in their path.

Drago took a moment to glance up at the sky. The moon was full. A good sign with the moon lighting their way to fortune. Drago turned to the others. "We'll see them better tonight."

A chorus of agreements came. Drago nodded to the side of the road and the men took up watch for the creatures that would soon make them richer than their wildest dreams. The fact that they would be destroying precious life in the process meant absolutely nothing to them. Greed was now fueling every inch of their brains. They sat and waited.

CHAPTER 4
CHAOS

A twig snapped near him and Thunder's ears perked up in surprise. He looked out at the elephants that were about a hundred yards away and found that they were all similarly startled. The herd stopped all activity and looked up.

Drago and his men peered out from behind a thick bamboo grove. Thunder turned just in time to see their silhouettes. While he may not have seen an upright before, he could tell that these creatures were not welcome near them.

"Huh?" His confusion was clear even to his own ears. Thunder saw darkness in the eyes of one man and gasped aloud. He raced away from the evil that dwelled within the depths of the upright that had intruded upon his safety.

Thunder picked up his pace, turning around repeatedly to see if the uprights were still there. He saw an opening in the tree line of the forest. Within that small hole, he could see Serenity across the watering hole. The men that were chasing him were also moving forward. He also saw several crouching low in the clearing surrounding the water hole.

A man whistled. Gunshots rang out, obliterating the silence of their peaceful night. Chaos and terror ensued, as

29

more cracking shots followed the first ones. Chimpanzees in the trees screamed in panic and scattered quickly into the highest depths of the canopy. The bonobos monkeys leapt higher into the branches, their curiosity no longer piqued, as fear had replaced it so easily.

A baby mongoose cried out to its mother. The mad fray inside the forest had made him lose sight of her. He raced through the bushes, anxiously searching for her with terrified shrieks.

The birds above Thunder squawked. Hornbills and pepper birds fluttered into the darkness, scrambling to hide in the recess of the dark canopy.

Thunder heard an agonizing scream as one elephant fell. Others fled the scene, doing their best not to trample the few that had fallen. Thunder saw flashes of moments pass before his eyes. He was not able to piece it all together. It was like a nightmare had replaced the peace he had always known. Fight or flight had kicked up in full gear, which made processing the moment even harder. He heard a female elephant moan and cry out, but wasn't able to make out her words. Thunder prayed that it was not his mother.

More gunshots pierced the air and Thunder froze in his tracks as he tried to determine what had made such a terrifying sound. "What is that?" He called out to the others, but no one answered.

Bang! Rip! Crash! Small bursts of light were erupting in the air near the uprights. He heard the men shout. Thunder tried to make out what was happening around him, but dust was blocking his vision. With limited visibility, Thunder could not see Serenity anywhere. He called out to her in a desperate plea, "Mom!!"

Branches scrape against Thunder's torso as he raced

through the forest, but he ignored the sharp pains. Palm fronds slapped him in the face and Thunder still continued on. He had to find Serenity.

Drago was now squatting in the forest, holding back from the wild chaos in the field. From his vantage point, he saw the baby elephant he had seen earlier and a plot formed in his head. While the adults would be used for their tusks, a calf could also be worth money. Perhaps a zoo or circus might want him. From here he looked like easy pickings. "I can sell him to the highest bidder." He rubbed his hands together in glee. "He won't get far. I'll get him."

The evil in his heart served him well. Tonight, Drago would get a good pay load for sure. He stood up and continued after the elephant, he had decided that this tiny elephant would be his spoil, if he could keep him separate from the other poachers. Double pay out, indeed.

A little further away, Penelope, an inquisitive, light-hearted parrot, entertained herself inside her nest. She had decorated her little abode with mirror shards she found washed up on the beach, as well as her prized possession. Her one and only book.

Penelope looked at herself in one of the mirrors suspended inside her nest. She whistled at herself and made cooing sounds as she crooned. A glass jar filled with fireflies sat nearby.

Penelope perused the book before her. The title on the

spine read 'Birds of a Feather.' She glanced inside the pages, as if this were a normal every day thing for a bird to be doing.

Merrily she said to herself, "What-a-ya-readin'? What-a-ya-readin'?" Penelope was used to having only herself for company. She spent many a day having conversations that only she would find amusing.

Penelope glanced at her reflection in one of the mirror shards and caught herself off guard. "Peekaboo. Peekaboo."

Penelope laughed aloud. Then she yawned, put the book down, and removed the glasses. "Hello, friend. Where'dya go? Where'dya go? Wooooo."

Penelope inched closer to one of the mirrors. "Aahh. Penelope. Penelope. Hello, friend. How ya doin'? Woohoo!"

The mirror image seemed to reply. "Welcome back. Welcome back. Are you lonely?"

She squawked quietly then responded to her image. "Hello, friend."

Her tongue made a clicking sound against the roof of her beak, before the mirror answered.

"Yippee!"

Penelope tilted her head at herself. "Will you stay with me? Will you stay with me? Pleeease."

Apparently her mirror image was just as lonely for a companion. "Never leave. No."

A low whistle rang out and the mirror shards all revealed the parrot's reflection. Each one took turns squawking at the other and throwing kisses back and forth. The parrot sat in the silence with herself, having a grand old time.

CHAPTER 5
CAPTURE

Thunder raced through the jungle. Ahead of him, he noticed a small light in a tree. He approached it hoping that he could find help out of his current situation. As it stood, he was alone trying to make sense of the events that had just unfolded. He had never been alone before and found he didn't like it at all. All Thunder wanted to do was find his mother and feel her warm embrace again.

Penelope heard a branch rustle below her. She muttered to herself, "Someone's there. Answer the door. Answer the door."

Nudging her jar of fireflies, Penelope waited for their light to give her better sight. The glow from the fireflies brightened the darkness around her. She picked up the jar with her wings, and carried it like a candle to her nest's door. She unlatched the door and peered skeptically down below through the branches of the tree.

A mild breeze cast shadows from the limbs as they swayed in the moonlight. Penelope scanned carefully and playfully called out. "Peekaboo. Peekaboo. Who's there? Woohoo!"

Crickets chirped, but soon stopped. The air became eerily

quiet. Penelope could not see much in front of her. "Is anyone there?"

The parrot noticed what looked like a large boulder covered with branches. This had not been there earlier today. When it moved slightly, her heart just about leapt out of her chest as she hopped back a step. "How ya doin'?" She made a clicking sound with her tongue and waited for a reply.

When none came, Penelope continued, "Come for a visit?" She whistled loudly and bobbed her head back and forth on her shoulders. "Time for dinner?"

The bulky object moved again, but did not reply. Her eyes peered into the darkness. "Come and see me."

Penelope made kissing sounds and bobbed her head again. "Come and see me."

Now more curious by the moment, the gray parrot stepped outside her door. Sneaking behind the tree trunk, Penelope peeked out and saw Thunder's head. "Elephant. Big feet. Long trunk. Woooo!"

From beneath the tree, Thunder finally heard her. "I'm down here!"

"Peekaboo," she replied.

"Hey!" Thunder looked up at her.

Penelope clucked her tongue against her beak and ruffled her feathers. "Hay is for horses."

Glancing into the tree branches, Thunder squinted for a better look. "I'm Thunder. I lost my herd!"

Penelope tilted her head from one side to the other as she stared at him. "Thunder? Thunder? Where's lightning?" The parrot whistled then cackled loudly at herself.

Thunder grumbled. "That's not funny!"

"Not funny, not funny."

Thunder attempted to ignore the mocking in the secretive

voice. "Can you help me?"

Penelope replied in her singsong voice, "What-a-ya' doin'?"

"A terrible thing happened!" Thunder felt tears running down his face as his voice trembled.

Penelope sensed his sadness. "Trouble. Everything okay, dear?" She made small kissing noises in an attempt to comfort him.

"Far from it! Where are you, mystery voice?"

Penelope waddled out from behind the tree branch. "Peekaboo. I see you."

Thunder let out a sigh of relief. "I see you."

"Nice to meet you," she replied.

At that moment, down on the ground near Penelope's tree, a human hand loaded a dart into a tranquilizer gun. The upright, Drago, raised the tranquilizer gun and pulled the trigger. Thunder groaned when the dart hit his skin. After a few seconds, the lights started to fade from before his eyes and he slumped over.

Penelope heard a loud thump and felt the tree shake in the darkness. Then all she could hear was a brutal silence. Peering down, she saw Drago standing near Thunder's limp body.

The upright glanced up, saw the parrot, and quickly decided she was another opportunity for financial gain. He reached behind him and pulled out a burlap sack, which he threw over her.

Penelope squawked fearfully before everything went black.

The next morning, Drago was traveling down the long dirt

road, his truck filled with his captives from the night before. Birds and animals lined the back of the truck bed in cages that kept them trapped securely inside. The small elephant calf was held inside the largest one. Drago knew this was only a temporary holding for the calf. Soon, he would auction him off to the highest bidder.

His goals of a rich future distracted him as he traveled over the bumpy road. His speed was far from safe, but Drago was not concerned. He had places to be, and people to bleed money from.

The green tree frog watched from the side of the road as the caged animals bounced perilously inside the strange vehicle. He choked on the trail of smoke that wafted from the truck's exhaust as it sped by him. He hopped away from the sight, shaking his head at the commotion.

Thunder started to regain consciousness, but his head was heavy and he felt groggy. He looked around in confusion as he struggled to grasp what was happening to him, but he was still completely disoriented. He blinked his eyes together a few times, attempting to clear the filmy haze that had collected over them.

A loud yowl of truck brakes filled the air and the squeaky, metal cages rubbed against each other. Thunder felt the cold metal meld against his skin and shook his head. He gazed at the bars and tried to make sense of it. He was trapped inside some kind of metal box. Looking over at the other cages, he saw several more captives.

Thunder's head bounced up suddenly when a shot rang out, loud like the ones from the night before. His world spun crazily as his heart pounded a mad rhythm in his chest. Then he heard several more shots follow the first. His head dropped back down to the floor of the cage. A tear slipped down his cheek. How had he managed to get himself in this mess? Thunder heard birds shrieking in terror. Monkeys wailed in the distance. Lifting his head again, Thunder could see them racing around as they attempted to avoid capture too in their wild panicked hysteria.

Thunder let out a long, tired sigh as he tried to keep his eyes open. He knew it wasn't wise to sleep, but he was still too tired to fight it. The last thing he saw before his eyes drifted closed again was a large, heavy tarp that concealed a mound of covered items.

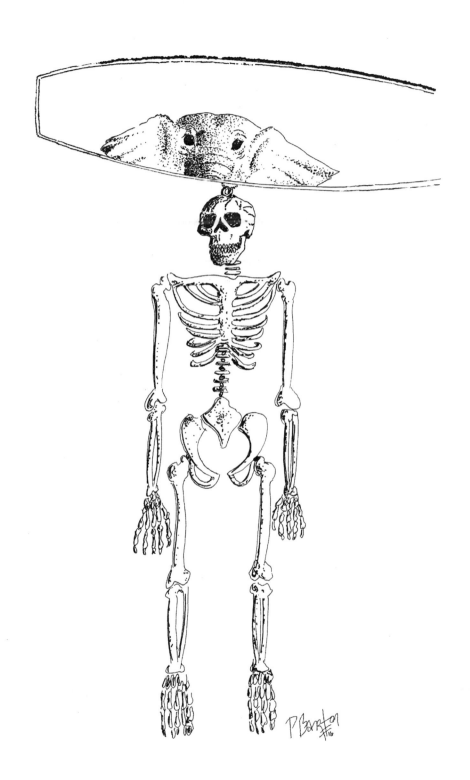

CHAPTER 6
CRASH!

From inside the burlap sack, Penelope was just beginning to stir. She lifted her wings, trying to free herself from the material holding her down. She stood up and hopped a few times, before her body bounced all around the cage. Her muffled voice called out, "Let me out. Let me out. Craauugghh!"

Upon hearing the parrot's quandary, Thunder stuck his trunk into the cage next to him. Picking the sack up, he gently wriggled it open and dumped Penelope out onto her cage floor. "There you go."

Penelope teetered on her feet for a moment before looking him directly in the eye. "Whew! Out! No bag for Penelope."

Thunder touched Penelope gently on the shoulder. "You're welcome, little bird."

Penelope took in her surroundings. "Uh-oh. Uh-oh. Not home."

Thunder replied, "It's not heaven. That's for sure."

"No heaven. Not home. Big trouble. Whhoooo!!" Penelope brushed the dust from her feathers. She was attempting to bring some sense of composure to herself, when Thunder's trunk sucked her up like a vacuum hose in an attempt to help her out.

Penelope's voice was muffled when she called out. Her wings fluttered wildly around her. "Aaahhh!! Unplug the parrot."

Penelope wrapped her wing around a bar of the cage and tried to yank herself from his grasp. Thunder pulled his trunk back, and Penelope fell from his grasp hitting the bottom with a loud thud. She rubbed her head and gave him a reproachful glance.

Thunder ducked his head from her gaze. "Sorry."

They sat there in the silence as the truck continued to wind down the long dirt road. Each one of them was thinking about how they could possibly get free from this impossible situation.

The upright, Drago, sat at the steering wheel inside the cab of the truck. He was whistling some tune oblivious to the plight of the animals in the cages in the back. His driving was becoming more reckless, the more he thought about the treasures that would soon be his. The weighted down truck dodged potholes and ruts, creating mass chaos in the back as cages rattled and squeaked relentlessly.

With the extra weight in the back, the truck struggled up the hill. Drago stepped on the gas as he texted on his phone. He did not notice the steep turn to his right. The truck veered dangerously close to the cliff's edge. Drago corrected his mistake by over steering to compensate. This was a huge mistake as the heavy unbalanced trucked tipped over and started a mad tumbling dash down the ravine.

Cages tumbled out from the truck, spilling open all over the ground in haphazard heaps of fur, fluff, and scales. Steam gushed from the radiator in front and hissed into the air menacingly. The animals scurried off and the birds flew away from the wreckage.

A spare tire flew off the truck and ran right over Penelope as she stepped out of her spilled cage. Thunder's cage also tumbled out, opened, and rolled away from the overturned truck, burying Penelope beneath its path. She was temporarily buried.

When the air became clearer, Penelope popped out from under the dirt. Now in complete disarray, she spit the sand from her mouth. "Pft! Pft! Pft!"

Thunder pushed up from his place on the ground. Quickly, he checked around to see where the upright was. Peering inside the truck, he saw Drago was still attached firmly to his seat. The upright appeared to be only semi-conscious at the moment. Out of the corner of his eye, Thunder saw the ivory skeleton swinging from the rearview mirror inside. His breath caught in his chest. He had never seen ivory anywhere else than the tusks that were worn proudly by the adult elephants in his herd.

Trying to ignore the dread in the pit of his stomach, Thunder gathered his wits and raced over to Penelope. He hovered over her, motionless, as he checked her for injuries.

Penelope put her feathers back in order, then looked up at him with fear in her eyes. "Not alone. Not alone."

Thunder nodded at her. "Not alone…but we're lost."

Penelope searched his eyes. "Just you and me. Wooo."

Thunder was about to reply, but at that moment the embankment he was standing on collapsed beneath his feet. Thunder tumbled down the hill and came to a rough halt against a downed log.

Penelope followed him and landed nearby. "How ya doin'?"

"Ah! I'm stuck! My leg!!" Thunder tried to pull his leg out, but the log against him would not budge.

Penelope made a high-pitched squeal that sounded very much like a rescue siren. She leapt onto Thunder's leg and tried to help him out.

Thunder pulled again, but no luck. He grunted loudly and tried again. "It's no use, I'm stuck."

Penelope shook her head sadly. "Tight spot. Big wood."

The two of them looked at each other hopelessly, each one wondering how they were going to get Thunder out of this situation before the upright came to full consciousness.

Chapter 7
Soma and the Egrets

A loud snorting could be heard near where Thunder was trapped. Penelope looked up at him with fear in her eyes. "Uh-oh."

Thunder trembled a little when he heard the snorting again. He had never heard anything quite like that before. "What was that?"

Penelope shook out her wings and stepped back a little. "Uh-oh. Gotta go. Not good."

The snorting came again and this time Thunder heard the sound of giggles accompanying it. He watched closely and swore his eyes were playing tricks on him. He did a double take and found that his imagination was not messing with him. A small cattle egret named Cedric was being tossed into the air. The tiny bird remained in the air, momentarily suspended. The tuft of feathers on his head was sticking out and his broad rounded wings were open.

Thunder continued to peer closer and found that there was a large, grayish mammal shrouded in the bushes. "It's one of us!"

Thunder heard repeated short air sounds. PFF. PFF. PFF.

He watched in surprise as the egret fell back down and landed on Soma, a female rhino with a broken horn. Two other egrets, Sydney and Persius, rested on her head and tickled her nose with a feather.

When Cedric swooped down and landed on Soma, Sydney changed places with him. The egret was puffed into the air just like her friend. She giggled louder than Cedric, enjoying every moment of her flight in the air. As she came down, Persius followed.

Cedric tapped Soma on the back with the tip of his white feathered wing. "Do it again! Do it again, Ms. Soma!"

Sydney squealed above them. "Higher! Woohoo!! Higher!"

Persius chuckled. "You're in rare form today, Ms. Soma!"

Soma did not respond in words. Instead she puffed up and sneezed. Each time she did so, the egrets flew into the air.

Thunder grunted at the playing group. "What fun! I wanna play!" He grunted annoyingly. "But I have to get my leg free!"

Soma, hearing Thunder, whipped her massive head around, causing the one egret in the air to crash to the ground like a rug pulled out from under him. Soma saw Thunder close to them and snorted loudly. She looked fierce, defensive, and ready to charge anything that moved.

The monkeys in the trees gathered above to watch the action below. They peered down from the perch making bets on how long the elephant calf would survive against the cranky rhino.

Thunder screamed and tried to get loose. Fear of the giant rhino gave him the extra boost he needed. He pulled so hard, his body bumped into a tree behind him. "Ahh! Ow!"

The egrets leapt up, startled momentarily, but when they

determined Thunder was no real threat to them, they landed back on Soma's torso.

Cedric was annoyed. He shook a wing at Thunder. "Hey! Hey!"

Sydney eyed him skeptically. "What are you doin'?"

Persius was still on the ground. He rubbed his head grumpily. "Givin' us a fright!"

"Yeah! You just can't sneak up on someone like that!" Sydney admonished Thunder.

"Yeah!" agreed Cedric heartily.

Soma faced Thunder, scraped the ground with her hooves and charged at the elephant calf. She stopped herself short when Thunder's scared voice trembled. "I'm sorry. I...I..."

Soma gave him a stern look as she towered over him "What are you doing here?"

Thunder tried to stand up tall and brave before her. "I thought you were an...."

Soma interrupted him. "A what"

Thunder answered quickly. "An elephant."

Soma shook her head at him. "Hmph. Likely story."

Thunder gave her a shy glance. "I'm looking for my herd."

She scoffed at him. "Your herd? You, sir, are trespassing!"

"I am? I thought I was just out for a walk." He offered the only excuse that came to his mind.

"Not around here. This is *my* territory." She snuffed in annoyance.

"Better watch this one, Ms. Soma. He's been out in the sun too long!" Cedric warned her.

"Just move along, you! Go back to your herd before you get us all in trouble." Soma kept her stone cold on Thunder.

Persius gave Thunder a sympathetic glance. "Oh, Ms. Soma. He's just a little tyke."

Sydney agreed with him. "Whoa. Give 'em a break."

Soma shook her head stubbornly. "Bah!" The rhino huffed in annoyance then grabbed a branch near her. She yanked it off with her teeth and started to chew on it.

A tear rolled down Thunder's cheek. "I was just trying to find my mom and my herd!" Thunder added dejectedly.

Soma grumbled, ignoring Thunder's sorrow, and continued to chew. Her mouth easily crushed the branch and she grabbed another.

Thunder sighed, wishing he could move on and head back to his herd, but his leg was still thoroughly stuck.

A monkey named Cole was watching him from above. He was sitting with his two friends, George and Lenny. "Don't listen to her! She thinks she owns the place!"

"Yeah!" George agreed. He picked a bug from Cole's fur and plopped it in his mouth.

Thunder turned his face to Soma wondering for the first time why the rhino was out here alone. "But...where's your herd?"

Soma huffed loudly. "There is no herd."

Thunder glanced closer at Soma and saw her broken horn for the first time. He wondered what had happened to it. A rhino's horn was its greatest defense mechanism. Soma at one point would have used it to gore any predators bent on attacking her or others in her herd. "What happened?"

Soma snarled at him. "Stay back! I don't need any more attention. I've had enough intruders to last a lifetime!"

Thunder stepped as far back as he could with his foot still trapped under the trunk. "Sorry." While she may not have her horn intact, Soma was still quite frightening to a calf like Thunder. He backed away feeling dejected.

Cedric whispered to Soma, "Ahem. Aren't you being a bit

hard on the kid?"

Sydney and Persius both agreed. "Yeah! Yeah!"

"I have to be! Or else!" Soma answered.

Persius tilted his head and looked down his orange beak. His beady gold eyes were trying to understand why Soma had so much to fear from something so little. "Or else what?"

"More danger!!" Her answer wasn't the kind any of them wanted to hear.

Thunder's eyes got big and fear raced through him. He was not sure his system could stand any more shock in one day. If danger came, what would he do? He was trapped like a fly in a spider's web. He would be easy pickings if the upright found him.

Soma barreled through the bushes with the three egrets bouncing on top of her back. Careless to the struggles that worried the tiny elephant, she continued on her way.

Penelope swooped down onto the branch of the trunk covering Thunder's leg. "Woohoo! Old Beast." She flapped her wings at the retreating rhino and imitated her awkward movements through the bushes. Holding her beak up like Soma's broken horn, she piped up. "Whoa! Neanderthal." Shaking her beak in disgust, Penelope straightened her ruffled feathers, and then glanced at Thunder again.

"What is your name?" Thunder realized he had never gotten it before. At least the gray parrot was gracious enough to keep him company through his troubled times.

Penelope tilted her sharp beak and answered, "Penelope. Penelope. Whatcha doin'? Peekaboo, who are you?"

"Thunder." He tried to free himself again, but still no luck. He pounded one of his free legs on the ground and the earth shook.

This caught the rhino's attention quite easily. Soma backed

up, snorted, and rumbled toward him. Clearly, Soma was not in the mood to play any games. Penelope moved from sight as fast as her parrot wings could carry her.

Thunder's eyes widened in fear. "Aauugghh! I'm sorry, I'm sorry!" He covered his eyes before he even saw who was heading his way.

Soma hooked her horn under the log and tossed it carelessly away from him. She snorted at him and stepped back a few steps.

Thunder opened one eye and peered cautiously around him. When he saw Soma in front of him, he did not know whether to be thankful or afraid of what the animal would do next. He gave her the benefit of the doubt. "Ahhhh! Soma! It's you!! Thank you!"

Soma sniffed at him half in annoyance, the other half of her thawing just a little to the calf. She grumbled at him. "Hmph. Better be more aware of your surroundings."

"I know." He stood up and tested his feet. His leg wobbled slightly, before he straightened it.

Penelope called out from her hidden perch. "Whew! Safe now."

Soma and the egrets looked up, but none of them could find where the voice had come from. Cedric shook his head. "Yikes!"

"Who said that?! Come out and be seen!" Sydney held up her wings like imaginary fists, ready to tackle whatever foe came their way.

"Yeah! Come out or she'll spear you!" Persius called out.

Penelope peered out from behind the tree trunk, with one wing over her eyes. She lifted it up before responding. "Peekaboo. Peekaboo. Where are you?"

Soma backed up and turned in confusion. She grumbled.

"Where is that silly creature?"

Penelope called out playfully, "In the tree. In the tree. I seeeee you."

Soma eyed the tree speculatively. When she saw the gray parrot she was underwhelmed. "Are you talking to me, parrot?"

Penelope nodded her beak at Soma. "Yes. Talking to you, Penelope is." The parrot gave a wolf whistle. "Ru—ruuuuuu!"

Penelope hopped on one foot then the other in a silly little dance. When she saw the jagged broken horn on Soma's head, she stopped in her tracks. "Big weapon. Sharp edges. Be carrreful!"

Soma shrugged her ears back in defense and huffed at the parrot. "I have to be fierce! I have my reasons, you know."

Sydney defended the rhino beneath her. "Yeah, she has her reasons!"

Persius jumped on the bandwagon. He raised his wings as if to say put 'em up. "Yeah, that's right! Soma has her reasons and we're three of them. Hah! Ha!"

Thunder watched the display before him and giggled at the sight. None of the animals were aware of how silly they appeared threatening a tiny parrot in a tree. Thunder took that moment to reach out to Soma and hug her with his trunk. "Thanks, Soma! You're my friend now, right? Mother always said never to tell your name to strangers, but you're not a stranger any more. I'm Thunder."

Soma grumbled and shrugged from his touch. "Meh. Enough with the feels already. So what? You're Thunder. Oh happy day!"

Cedric was now staring at the intruders with suspicion. "So what are you all doin' in these parts?"

Thunder answered him, "I'm trying to find my herd. Will

you help me? You can come with us."

The egrets turned and looked at each other with puzzled looks. Persius interrupted the silence. "Do we want to come?"

Cedric tilted his head at Persius. "I dunno. Do we?"

Sydney shook her head at her friends. She was always the daredevil of the bunch. She poked each one in the belly. "Oh don't be chickens. A great adventure awaits us."

Soma pawed the ground with her hoof. "Adventure, hmph. I've had plenty of adventure. Go away and leave me alone please. Adventure. Bah!" She grumbled more to herself than anyone else.

Persius tapped her head with his foot. "Aw, c'mon, big girl. We've got nothin' else to do."

"Why should I?" The rhino was old, cranky, and set in her ways. It would take a lot to persuade her at this point.

"Well, that's quite the attitude. When did you become such a cranky pants? We were just having a grand old time too." Cedric made a disappointed clucking sound at Soma.

Sydney's eyes flew open wide. She raised one feather in the air, as if to say she had a brilliant idea. "But, you know Ms. Soma, the elephants always find the best watering holes…and the best trees to munch off of. What-a-ya think?"

Persius caught on to Sydney's train of thought. It was far easier to tempt a fly with honey than vinegar after all. "Tempting, isn't it?"

Soma squinted an eye at Thunder as her thoughts churned in her head. "Where did you say you're headed?"

Thunder smiled at Soma, feeling hope for the first time since he was captured by the upright Drago. "To our watering hole! I know they're out there somewhere."

He waited to see if she would answer. When she did not, he continued, "You'll love meeting my mom and the rest of the herd. And there's birds, mud, salt..."

Soma interrupted Thunder. "Did you say mud? *And* salt?"

Thunder smiled all the way up to his big round eyes. "Yep."

"Hm." Soma was clearly thinking about her options now.

Cedric patted Soma on the head. "That's the spirit!"

Sydney cheered, "Let's go!"

Penelope peered at the animals below her. "Going home, dear? Yesssssss!"

Persius looked up at Penelope. "Where's *your* family?"

Penelope sniffed sadly. "All gone. Woooo."

A tear ran down Penelope's small feathered face. A memory welled up deep within her mind. She remembered a flock of carefree parrots picking up seeds from the forest floor. A giant fish net swung through the air and swallowed all them up.

The parrots had darted and dashed under the strong netting that held them close to the forest floor. Penelope got her foot stuck in the strings holding them close together. She remembered pecking at it, enough to squeeze through a tiny hole. She flew a few feet away from the net, while the other parrots remained trapped within its confines. Penelope stood there alone on the ground. Abandoned, hopeless, the parrot had no choice but to fly away and fend for herself.

Penelope dashed at the tears and shook away her memories. "Oooooo. Sad story. All alone now."

Persius tried to cheer her up. "Come with us! Parrots are great guides!"

Penelope answered him with a cocky reply. "Yes, Penelope is a parrot. Pretty, pretty parrot." She looked away from them and started to preen her feathers.

Sydney waved the bird closer. "Well, here's your chance!"

Soma shook her head. Her grouchiness had returned. "Make up your minds, feather brains. I don't have all day, you know." She nodded for Thunder to lead the way and he started to walk slowly in the direction where he had last seen his herd. Penelope flew from the branch and settled on a branch several feet ahead of them. The animal party continued through the bushes in easy silence, at least for the moment.

CHAPTER 8
STARVING

A poor African farmer named Mosi was driving his rusty pickup home after returning from a long day of work. While he was young, in his thirties, Mosi often felt as if he were old and gray. He reached inside the backend of the truck and grabbed a small cloth sack. It contents were meager, and certainly not enough to keep his small family fed. Mosi walked up to the small rusty shack where he lived with his wife, Sarani, four-year-old daughter, Imani, and their tiny baby.

As he got closer, Mosi heard the young squalls of the hungry baby inside. His daughter was playing just outside the door with her dog, Senji, a Basenji puppy. He ruffled Imani's head with his hand and took in the goofy, bright smile she gave him. It lifted his spirits slightly.

Mosi opened the door and stepped inside. The room inside the shack was filled with different sounds. The old electric fan spinning and buzzing overhead sputtered as it turned slowly. The crying baby was not one to be drowned out though. Mosi saw Sarani sweat soaked from the sweltering heat and felt his failures coming to light again. He worked harder than most men and still could not keep his wife the way he thought she deserved. Handing her the bag, he watched as Sarani dumped out its contents.

Tears welled up in her eyes as she saw the handful of carrots and potatoes that had been stashed inside. This would never be enough to feed their tiny family. "Is this all there is?"

Mosi looked away from her. He no longer felt man enough to meet her eyes. "Yes, I'm afraid so."

"All of this…these measly vegetables? How will we ever feed our family of four? Mosi, what are we going to do?" Tears gave way to hollow sobs that wracked her tiny, starving frame.

Mosi couldn't handle the despair in Sarani's voice. "I will go out to the farthest field. Maybe it's untouched. Then I will go to the village and look for something to cool you off with."

Mosi leaned over and kissed Sarani on the forehead. He rubbed a gentle finger over the top of his infant son's head and took a deep breath. "I will be back soon."

"Please hurry, Mosi. I don't feel well." Sarani looked paler than usual to him. He must hurry to find something that would bring her relief. He would do whatever it took.

As the door closed behind him, Mosi wiped the sweat off his face and neck with his sleeve. Imani was now playing in the yard with Senji. He waved at her before he went back to his beat up truck. When he turned the key in the ignition, the engine would not start. After numerous tries, he hit the steering wheel with both hands and angry tears welled up in his eyes. "Not again! Aaarrgghh! Can just one thing go right?"

He got out of the truck and slammed the door. Walking around the side of the shack, Mosi retrieved his bicycle from the tool shed next to it. He jumped on it and pedaled his way down a dirt path that led to their crops.

Imani smiled and waved at him. "Bye, Papa!"

Mosi did not reply. He heard Senji bark close to him, but he paid the aimless puppy no mind as he continued to make his way further toward the fields.

He rode along a wire fence on his plot of land, stopping abruptly when he saw a herd of elephants. From here he could see that most of the crops had been trampled or eaten. "Nooooo!!"

Jumping off his bike, Mosi jogged along the path outside the fenced in land, waving his arms in an effort to scare off the large pachyderms. "Get out!! Get out!! Shoo! Shoo!!" He shouted at them.

The elephants raised their trunks and splayed back their ears, but did not move an inch.

Mosi was furious as he hustled back to his bicycle. He hopped on and rushed off trying to figure out how he was going to feed his family if a herd of elephants had taken every inch of the food he had left to give.

The next morning, Mosi left the shack as soon as he could and headed straight into the village. People were bustling about the marketplace. Some were shopping at the outdoor market.

Mosi rode through the village. People were out and about, shopping at outdoor stalls that were filled with handmade crafts and home grown produce. He watched some of them as they delivered merchandise to their stalls.

Jumping off his bicycle, he raised his hands to draw attention to himself. "The elephants!! They're back!! Elephants!! Hurry!!"

The villagers stopped their activities and turned to look

at Mosi. Some started to gather around him. A few eyed him speculatively, as if to say what do you expect us to do about it.

Mosi shouted over a slow murmuring of voices. "They're back... the big beasts! And they are hungry!!"

Drago had been watching the crowd gather around Mosi. When Mosi started going on about elephants, his eyebrow rose curiously. He rubbed his hand gently over the Band-Aid that was covering his head. The crash had really knocked him senseless for a while. The worst part was that he had lost all the valuable animals he had trapped that day.

Mosi kept speaking to the crowd passionately. He did not want to hurt the beasts, he only wanted to find a way to work together with the village to problem solve the situation. "They are ruining our crops! Now, we have no money to feed our families! No future!"

Someone in the crowd shouted, "They must be stopped!"

Drago turned to the voice and added his thoughts to fuel the fire that was burning slowly in the crowd. He saw the wheels turning. He knew it was his chance. "Yeah! And they ruined my new truck!"

An older man in the crowd shouted, "They should be put in a zoo!"

The others gathered around them shook their heads in agreement. More low murmuring erupted in the crowd. A young man shouted his agreement. "Yeah! Yeah! Lock those beasts up!"

Mosi shook his head at the people before him. With them on his side, he could get the elephants away from his land. He might have to replant, but eventually the crops would grow and his family would survive once again. "They need to go!!"

Drago stepped up to Mosi and pulled him aside. He whispered in his ear, "If you do what I do, you will be fine and have a good life, cousin."

Mosi looked at his cousin. He knew the kind of man Drago was. Drago was a poacher who made his money off the various body parts of animals that others had deemed valuable. Mosi did not want to destroy the elephants the way that Drago did, but he did want to survive. Right now, those elephants were standing in the way of their survival. "I don't know, Drago." He shook his head at him slowly.

Drago gave him a crooked smile. "Well, you'll know soon enough when your baby gets sick and your wife weeps for you to do something."

Mosi wanted to shake off the fear rising within him. What Drago said was true. Both of those things could happen and there was very little he could do to stop them. Mosi had created the murmur of dissonance among his people. It was easy to see that no clear resolution would happen at this moment. He waited around to see where the crowd would lead, all the while praying Sarani would in better spirits when he returned home.

CHAPTER 9
FRIENDS

At the bottom of the hill, Thunder was leading the group through the rainforest. There was no time to waste if he was going to find his mother. "C'mon. I have to get back to my herd."

Penelope queried from the trees. "No herd? No herd?"

Thunder shook his trunk at her and rolled his eyes. The parrot picked a small twig from the branch above him and dropped it on his head. "Stop goofin', Penelope. I have to find them."

Penelope shuffled her feet on her perch and wobbled her head from side to side. "Go home now. Go home. Dinner waiting. Can't get cold."

Cedric pruned his feathers with his dagger shaped beak, while he held onto Soma's back gently with his feet. He glanced up at Penelope and smiled. "Stick with us!"

Sydney shook her head ruefully at her friend. She couldn't care less if Penelope the parrot came with them anywhere. That bird's antics were seriously grating on her nerves. She'd already made that loud and clear. "Speak for yourself, Cedric!"

Persius jabbed Sydney in the stomach and shook his head

reproachfully. "Be nice, Sydney."

"Hey!! Ouch! Stop it, will ya! Ow!!" Sydney hopped to the side to avoid another poke from Persius and tumbled from Soma's back. The small egret landed in a heap behind the rhino and looked up to see Soma's tail swishing in her face. She blew the tail from her beak and gave a loud disapproving huff of air. Sydney raised her left wing in the air and pointed at Persius. "Just you wait, you!"

"Or what? You'll knock my stuffing out?" If Persius had a tongue, he would have stuck it out at her. Instead, he settled for splaying the feather tips of his wings out around his beak and shaking his head at her tauntingly.

"I will, just you wait!"

Thunder stomped on the ground and Sydney shook slightly, making a small vibrating chirping sound as all the air left her lungs. "Look, we have to work together if we're going to get back to my herd. Team work. Got it?"

Soma stopped mid-step and looked first at Sydney, then the elephant calf in front of her who was acting like more than just their glorified tour guide. "Oh brother. Now we have a committee. What's next? The U.N.?" Soma began to imagine a herd of elephants waving patriotic flags to the backdrop of some big band song that made them stamp their feet in rhythm. She shook the image away, deciding that these loony animals must be getting to her.

Thunder turned and faced Soma square on. "I can't do it by myself. I'm afraid they'll get me."

Soma could not ignore the watery eyes staring back at her, or the slight tremble of fear in Thunder's voice. She understood him more than he knew. Soma had gone through much at the hands of the uprights. Their impression was left on her to this day. She shrugged off the welling of emotions racing through her. Pitying the calf would not help him in the least. It was better he learned now how cold the world could be. "Well, kid, get used to it. Survival of the fittest, ya know?"

Penelope flew to a limb closer to them and rotated her head from side to side. "Darwin. Great man."

Soma grumbled. "Yeah, yeah, yeah." She really had no idea what the silly bird was going on about now. Not that it mattered. Her bird brain was the least of their worries. Soma nodded to Thunder, "Let's keep moving."

Thunder looked as if he were going to say something, but thought better of it. He waited for Soma to reach his side and they proceeded together in quiet.

Penelope dove from the trees and perched precariously on his head. She tilted her head at the egrets on top of Soma's back as if to say who has the better ride now? A rustling sounded near them and Penelope hopped up and down excitedly. "What's up? Uh-oh. Someone at the door." She ended with a shrill whistle that made the other birds cringe.

Sydney looked all around them in confusion. "What door?"

"Knock, knock. Who's there?" Penelope quipped in her singsong voice.

The animals stopped briefly, and turned around to scan the area. An unusual silence blanketed the forest. Not a single animal made a peep. That was certainly cause for concern. Soma raised her head and sniffed the ar. "It's not safe here. Keep moving."

"Oh, goodie! Does that mean we're along for the ride?" Cedric asked. While the egrets had been with Soma for a few days, there was never a guarantee of how long Soma would let them stay around her. The grumpy rhino was awfully selective sometimes.

Soma sniffed in exaggerated irritation. "I suppose. If you must."

Sydney cheered, "All right then!"

Persius did a little happy dance on Soma's back. "Let's go! Boogey down! Woo-woo!"

Penelope began to do a little dance on Thunder's head. She bobbed her head up and down and shuffled her feet from side to side. "Nothing to lose."

Soma rolled her eyes at the tiny creatures. "I hope we're home for dinner."

Penelope must have agreed with Soma's words. She squawked once then added, "Home for dinner. Okay. Set the table."

Thunder cheered at Penelope. "Yay, Penelope!"

The parrot pointed to the east enthusiastically. "Let's go fly!" She slid down Thunder's trunk and flew up into the trees. She skipped from tree to tree. "Wheeeee!"

Thunder continued along, taking a few steps in front of Soma when the path before them became narrower. Soma trailed behind him at steady pace. The egrets bobbed up and down on the rhino's back grabbing up the insects as they landed on Soma and gobbling them up before they could fly away.

Cedric swallowed a tasty treat. "Mmm."

Sydney gulped up hers. "Tasty! Needs salt though."

Persius sucked up a few smaller insects that were trying to evade him. "I just can't get enough!"

The group continued to make their way through the rainforest in amiable silence, searching for Thunder's herd and their next big meal. The rumbling of Soma's stomach competed with Thunder's, but they continued on their way ignoring the hunger that called out to them.

CHAPTER 10
LEOPOLD

As they passed by a bush, a low rumble turned into a large growl. A large male leopard was hiding within the leafy branches, so well camouflaged that Thunder almost didn't see him. Thunder jumped back slightly and his front legs lifted into the air in alarm. Every inch of the elephant calf was trembling. He had never seen a leopard before, but he had certainly heard of them.

Soma froze in her tracks then found a spot in the large overgrowth near her. The rhino lowered her head, prepared to ram the leopard from her position if the need arose. The egrets, which had been waddling next to them, jumped up from the ground and landed on Soma's back. As soon as they landed on her back, Sydney pushed Cedric to the front.

"Get off, will ya?" Cedric pulled Sydney in front.

"Hey, lay off." She moved behind Persius, whose eyes were almost bulging out of his head.

"M-m-mee?? You want me to be in front? I'm not brave!" He pulled Sydney next to him and locked his wing with hers. "If I have to be here, so do you!"

"Chicken," muttered Sydney.

"Look who's talking!" Persius stomped his foot on hers and hooted in laughter when she loosened her grip, jumped up and down with her wings grabbing her foot, and ultimately landed ahead of the other two egrets.

Leopold the leopard eyed the spectacle and rolled his eyes to the sky above him. It was hard to keep his predator stance with the mockery in front of him. He snarled low and deep to get the birds' attention and all three of them stood stock still.

Thunder backed up and worried about what he should do. Amidst the opening of leaves, he could now see the cat more clearly. The creature in front of him was a good sized jungle cat with a creamy yellow coat that faded to white from his stomach down to his toes. Every inch of the leopard was covered in black half-circle spots that reminded him of a small hoof print. The cat's long whiskers trembled as he opened his mouth to expose his sharp fanged teeth that could easily rip apart any animal in seconds. Thunder closed his eyes and prepared to cringe.

Penelope the parrot chose that moment to return to the group. She had flown away on some flighty mission only she understood. Landing on the branch above them, her golden eyes sparkled. "Someone's here. Someone's here. Hmmm. Leopard." Penelope chirped like a bird for a moment then mimicked a low growl like the beast below her. "Neee— owwwwwwwwww!"

Leopold relaxed his posture, sat back on his haunches and examined his right paw as he pretended disinterest in the animals before him. "Good evening."

Sydney did not trust Leopold one bit. "Oh-oh."

Persius craned his head toward the bush. "C-c-c-come out where we can see you."

Leopold spoke slow and deliberately. "Is this a little lost

elephant I see here with you or a scrumptious Friday night special? Oh, goodie, what a treat indeed."

Thunder backed up into a mangrove tree. His feet tripped over its thick, heavy roots and he fell on his backside. Covering his eyes with his large floppy ears, he tried to imagine himself anywhere but here.

Cedric squawked at the leopard. "No! This is Thunder, a pygmy elephant with a problem."

Leopold grinned to himself, thinking about what a tasty treat the little calf would make. "I'll say he has a problem."

Cedric held a wing up and shouted, "Stay back! Or Soma will rearrange your spots!"

Sydney crossed her wings in front of her and tapped one foot on Soma's back. "Or she'll re-connect your dots!"

Persius held up his wing, with one long feather pointing at the bush. "Yeah!"

Penelope's impish voice called out, "Where's the beef?"

Soma stepped forward from behind a bush. She pawed the ground with her hoof and a loud snuff of air left her nostrils. She was ready for attack. The egrets on top of her scrambled to the rear of her backside, each one huddled in fear.

Leopold shrugged his shoulders, a little put out that things were not going to go so easily for him. "Oh, all right, then. I guess dinner will have to wait."

Thunder lowered one of his ears from his eyes and peered cautiously around. He tried to stand up, but his foot caught in one of the tree roots and he rolled over onto his behind once more. He let his ears flap to the back of his head and this time when he stood, he avoided the pesky roots. He stood as tall as a frightened elephant calf could, with his whole body trembling in little shakes as he addressed the leopard. "Who... who are you?"

"Don't you know? I am Leopold." The leopard was shocked that the animals had never heard of him before this point. He was a legend in the forest, after all.

Soma shook her head in annoyance at the arrogant leopard. "We don't want any trouble. We're just trying to help this one out," she gestured to Thunder. "He's looking for home."

Leopold chose that moment to step out from the bushes. He walked around Thunder, much like a snake, his lanky body seeming to slither around him. When he came face to face with Thunder, he gave him a secretive smile. "Home? That's a curious concept out here in the wild."

Penelope peered out from her perch. She did not trust the leopard one bit. "Uh-oh. Wrong karma. Stay back."

"Hm. Very interesting. Is anyone expecting you?" Leopold was calculating the outcomes if he continued to pursue his quarry.

Thunder started to shake again. Leopold was definitely off-putting. He pointed ahead with his trunk. "Well, yes! My herd…a really *big* herd. They're just… they're over there!"

"Let me see then." Leopold turned toward Thunder, crouched low, and stalked him closer with his eyes and every inch of his body language. "And where did you say your herd was?"

Thunder shook off a shiver of fear. "You're not going to hurt me, are you?"

Leopold considered his options. "I don't know. What if I did?"

When the leopard moved around and stuck his menacing face in Thunder's, Soma huffed near them. She chaffed her front hooves on the ground and prepared to attack. "Don't even try it."

The egrets chimed in, each still huddled together.

Sydney shivered a little, her courage not as loud as usual. "Yeah!!"

Persius nodded at the leopard with his orange beak, "That's right!! We mean it! Don't even."

Leopold shook his head, sighed dramatically, then leapt onto a rock nearby. "That boy is not going to make it in the jungle."

Sydney feigned bravado. "Yeah, well, we'll see about that!"

From his safe perch on Soma's back, Persius was feeling brave. He wagged his wing tip at Leopold as the leopard darted off into the bushes. "Yeah, you overconfident kitty!"

Leopold decided his intended meal wasn't worth the rhino attack and slinked off into the jungle.

As life started to return around them, monkeys chattered above them, birds chirped and called to each other within the recess of the canopy, they watched to make sure the leopard had really gone.

"Coast is clear," Penelope squawked and flew from the branches above them to land on Thunder's head. "Homeward bound."

Soma continued to watch the spot the leopard had just vacated. "Pompous fool," she grumbled under her breath.

Cedric jumped up and down on Soma's back. "You showed him, Ms. Soma!"

"Yeah!" The other two chimed in.

Thunder joined Soma on the trail, still a little choked up over what had just happened. "You saved me." He ran his trunk over Soma's head. "Thank you."

Soma huffed, not liking the added attention. "You're making too much of this kid," she grumbled.

"Wooooo!" Penelope squawked again. "Homeward

bound. Find the herd. Late for dinner. Wooooo!"

The group resumed their quest to find Thunder's herd.

The group of traveling companions may have thought they were safer, but they had no idea that Drago and his men were pushing through the rainforest. The hunters traveling with Drago were whacking and slashing the plants everywhere around them with their long machete blades. Drago would not give up until he regained the treasures he had lost in his accident. If they continued their steady pace, they would eventually catch up to the elephant calf.

Drago let his greedy dreams take over his mind as he walked behind the hunters. This time he would buy a fancy new motorcycle, bright red with chrome accents. That would certainly raise his status in the village. Maybe a large plot of land? There were several farmers desperate for money to survive. He could buy the majority of them off their lands.

He continued to plot and plan as he plodded his way through the jungle. One thing was true. Drago never quit.

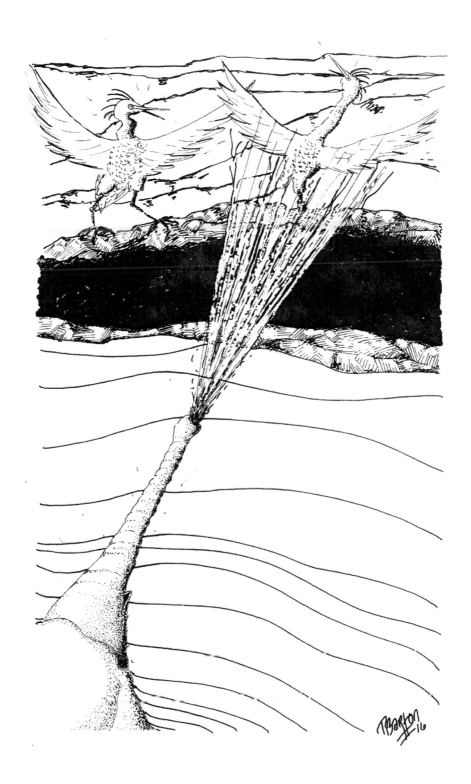

CHAPTER 11
GONE FOR A SWIM

As the group of mismatched animals traveled further through the jungle, Thunder stopped abruptly. He sniffed the air trying to find any clue of his herd. His tail swished and swatted a mosquito near his flanks. "Okay, Penelope, which way do we go?"

They had been relying on Penelope's tracking skills when Thunder no longer knew where they should go. "This way. Woohoo!!"

Penelope darted to a tree several yards ahead. She turned around to face them then cocked her head to one side. Her feathers shook ever so slightly as she rotated her head again. "Peekaboo. Hello friends. I see you."

Soma grumbled at the perky parrot. "Yes, yes. We see you. Now, let's get on with it already."

"Yeah, yeah, yeah," agreed Persius.

The animals continued to follow her, each one of them caught up in their own private thoughts.

From nearby, Drago peered out from behind a giant fern that kept him and his men hidden from view. He gestured for the hunters to stay down. "Look at that, will you?"

The hunter next to him whistled. "That's some mighty fine animals."

"Worth a fortune," agreed Drago. The only downfall was that Drago would have to split the profits with the others.

"Shall we attack them?"

"Not yet. Let's keep close. I have a feeling they my lead us to something greater. We'll stop here for now." Drago ordered. He watched the men find different spots around him to rest against small trees. Evening would fall before long. They would need to be at full energy in the morning if they were going to overtake the rhino and elephant calf. With that jagged horn, the rhino was not as valuable, but there would still be other uses for the beast. He smiled to himself, "Ah yes. The forest has endless treasures, and all for us to take!"

He propped himself up against a tree near him and crossed his arms over his chest. He fell asleep with a satisfied look plastered on his face.

Night had fallen over the jungle. Moonlight shone on the lake below as the rushing water from the falls above sent rings of waves all around the surface. A cave was nearly hidden next to the magnificent falls. Soma, Thunder, and the tiny white egrets were settled right before the cave entrance.

Penelope flew up to a fig tree nearby and started to peck at the fruit. "Yum, yum. Dinner."

Thunder walked over to the fig tree and rubbed his side up against it. When his movements shook the tree, Penelope leapt up. "Tree is dancing. Uh-oh. Earthquake. Take shelter!"

The tree rattled more and Penelope bobbed her head up and down excitedly. "Uh-oh! Oh my! Oh my! Uh-oh! We're going down!" She held up her wings like she was piloting a plane and made machine gun noises. "Rat-a-tat-tat-tat-tat-tat-tat!" The gray parrot fell from the top branch, latched onto the one below her and swung all the way up and around it twice before finally standing straight. "Whew!" The bird pulled herself together and shook off the leaves that had attached themselves to her feathers.

Thunder looked up at the mass of ruffled feathers peering anxiously over the branch. He gave her a goofy, apologetic grin and laughed softly. "Sorry, Penelope. It was me! I had an itch!"

"What-a-ya doin'? Shaking the tree. Uh-oh. No good."

Soma shook her head at the commotion and turned to look around them. She found a huge mud puddle next to the waterfall and it called to her. It was like a magnetic pull. Soma lumbered toward it with a big smile. "Ah! At last."

Cedric shuffled his feet from on top his perch on Soma's back. He suddenly felt a little nervous. "Where are you goin', Ms. Soma?"

Persius caught on to the anxious tone in Cedric's voice. He leaned over to get a better look in front of them. "Uh-oh. Bath time."

Sydney squawked. "Time to disengage, if you know what I mean!"

The three egrets flew off of Soma's torso and landed on Thunder who was shaking his head ruefully at their antics. Sydney sat down with her legs folded under and her wings stretched at her sides almost as if she were nesting on top of him. "Aahhh! Much better!"

Persius sighed. "And his skin is so soft! Like velvet!" The egret rubbed his face in Thunder's back. "Aaaah!"

Soma waded into the muddy water. It squished around her as she moved and she sighed with an almost goofy grin, the first that she had displayed in quite some time. Soma put her nose down to the mud and blew into it. Small bubbles appeared on the surface of the goo. Her tail flicked happily in the mud behind her, then flung a sticky mess into the air around her. Soma was in rhino heaven at the moment. Not a care in the world.

The parrot watched the rhino from her branch. "Mmm. Gone for a swim."

Thunder looked over where Soma was now rolling around in the mud. He noticed the pond next to the puddle. He walked closer to the waterfall and let some of the wandering sprays tickle his skin.

"Oh no! He's goin' in! Argh! Abandon ship!" Cedric warned. The egrets leapt up from his back and landed on a ledge above the cave opening.

Thunder watched the birds above him and shook his head. "You birds are weird. It's just a little water after all." He stepped into the small pond and let himself relax for the first time that day.

As he soaked in the cool pond, Thunder pondered the journey that had brought him here. The thought of the uprights with their weapons that boomed like thunder made him wonder if his name was as destructive as the fire that burst like lightning from their barrels. How could man be so vicious to creatures that were only trying to live in peace?

Thunder shook off the dire thoughts that circulated in his head. They were much too serious for one as young as he. They were ideas that he would never have had, if he and

77

his herd had been safe from the poachers. All he wanted now was to find his mother and he wondered if she were safe. Did Serenity find a way from the trucks, like he had?

Thunder lowered his trunk into the water and vacuumed water up. He lifted it up and sprayed the water against his back. He was reminded of the playful calves at the pond. He smiled and a new thought entered his mind. Thunder zeroed in on the egrets on top of the ledge and closed one eye as he got them within his sights.

"What-a-ya doin'?" Penelope called from above.

"Shhh, Penelope!" Thunder cautioned her.

The egrets were still chatting away to each other. They did not notice him until it was too late. Thunder shot the water at them and giggled when they fell back against the cave wall behind them. They gave him evil glares as they pruned the water from their feathers.

"No fair!" accused Sydney.

"Yeah, what's the big deal here?" Persius narrowed his eyes at Thunder.

"I suppose we needed a bath sometime." Cedric pointed out.

"Sorry. I couldn't resist." Thunder gave them a goofy grin.

"That's okay. We'll get payback eventually, elephant," Sydney promised.

Thunder turned back to the water and saw his reflection in the ripples below. "I wonder if they miss me."

Soma grunted in the puddle next to him. "You worry too much."

"Soma, would you miss me, if you were my mother?" Thunder felt another tear rolling down his cheek. He made a small snuffle sound as more tears came out.

Soma gazed out into the distance with a lonely stare. She

took a few moments to reply. "Yes, Thunder. I would miss you if you were mine."

Thunder sniffed. "Thank you, Soma."

"Now if you don't mind. I would like to enjoy my bath in silence."

"Right. Sorry." Thunder plopped down in the water and it almost reached his eyeballs. He let his trunk float on the water's edge and settled in to enjoy the quiet from his surroundings. From time to time, he saw the egrets whispering as they gestured toward him and he wondered what they were plotting.

CHAPTER 12
HARU

Thunder dipped his trunk in the water one last time, sprayed his head, and climbed out. He stood beneath the entrance of the cave and wondered what might be inside. "What's in here?"

Soma called from the mud, "Rhinos don't do caves."

The egrets agreed in a chorus, "And neither do we!"

Thunder poked his head inside the entrance. "Well, I do. Anything in here?" He heard his words echo a little and his eyebrows rose curiously.

"Hell-o. Hell-o. Hell-o!"

His words were tossed right back at him like careless whispers that reverberated over and over. "Cool! Hey, I can hear myself!"

Penelope swooped down onto Thunder's head and imitated Thunder. "Hell-o. Hell-o. Nobody home."

From inside the cave a voice could be heard. "The runway looks clear for take-off! Let's go, brothers!"

A group of bats scattered into formation as they streamed out of the cave above Penelope and Thunder. Thunder dove to the ground, covering his eyes with his floppy ears and

Penelope ducked under her wings.

The bats' wings flapped and a collective swoosh filled the air. The path of bats looked like one large black cloud.

Persius screamed from the top of the cave entrance. "Aahhh! Night riders!"

"Watch out! Low-flying jet!" warned Sydney.

Cedric ducked beneath his wings. "Shields up."

The egrets leapt from their roost at the top of the cave entrance and made a mad dash for a palm tree near them. They looked each other over from head to toe making sure that all their feathers were still in place.

One bat left the squadron and deviated to where Penelope and Thunder now stood gazing at them curiously. It landed abruptly in front of them, with his feet back pedaling to slow himself down. His speed was so great that he had trouble putting on the brakes. He landed in a heap right next to them, then pursed his lips and sucked a small insect into his mouth as if flew by.

The hyper black bat, named Haru, was blinking its tiny eyes at the elephant standing above him. His small ears rounded, and then formed tiny points at the top of his head. He lowered his black wings and bowed respectfully to them. "Helloooo."

Penelope tilted her head at the tiny bat. "Nice to meet you. Home for dinner?"

Haru gave them a goofy grin that showed his white pointy fangs. "On our way to dinner. I'm Haru. Who are you?"

"Penelope. Penelope's here. Pretty bird."

Haru offered her a wing to shake, but Penelope would not leave her perch on Thunder. He lowered his wing and sniffed softly. "Did you come for a visit?"

Penelope gazed at him curiously. Her head rotated in half

circles to the left and right. "Friend?"

Haru gave a huge smile. "We're all friends! And you?"

Thunder lowered his trunk to Haru's wing. "I'm Thunder."

"Thunder? Nice to meet you. Care for a bite?"

"I've eaten already. Thanks." Thunder nodded at the bat.

Penelope opened her beak a few times. "Yum, yum, yum, yum, yum. Dinner."

Penelope made the sounds of kisses being blown into the air. "Mu-mu-mu."

Soma climbed out of the pond to join them. She glared at Haru before pounding the ground. Her threat was clear.

Haru tilted his head at her. "You don't think every stranger's an enemy, do you? Hmm?"

Soma snorted. "In my world, yes."

"That's not how it's supposed to be! C'mon now!" Crossing his wings behind his back, Haru walked around in circles.

Penelope's eyes followed his circular movements and her head rotated around her neck. "Listen. Wheeee!"

Haru laughed at the silly parrot. "Yes, we are gentle creatures who love to have a good time — if you know what I mean!"

Haru looked up anxiously when he noticed the formation of bats above him, his ears perked up, and he no longer noticed the animals in front of him. Standing to attention, he saluted the sky and called to the squadron of bats above him, "Radar up and operational, sir!"

Thunder turned to Soma. "What's he doing?"

Soma had no answer for him. She had no idea what the goofy bat was up to. She stood there with a blank stare as her answer.

"Standard procedure, soldiers," answered Haru.

The egrets were now leaning over their tree branch to listen. Persius was the first to speak. "Who's he talking to?"

"I dunno," Sydney answered.

Cedric shook his head in confusion. "Are we in the middle of an air force base or what?"

Sydney shrugged her shoulders. "Someone should tell 'em the war's over."

"What war?" Persius asked.

Cedric shook his head at him. "Never mind."

"You only come out at night?" Thunder asked Haru.

"Man, that's the best time! It's all stars in the night sky! See?" He nodded his pudgy nose to the stars that peeked from the vivid blue canvas of the night sky.

Haru sucked up another insect flying by him. "Thwp!!"

Pointing upwards with one of his wings, he blinked. "Come with us! We'll show you!"

Thunder tilted his head at the loony bat. How could he possibly? "I'll stay on the ground, thank you."

"Suit yourself," Haru said.

"Night flight?" Penelope raised her voice to a higher squealing pitch. "Yippee!!"

"Yes!! Follow me!" Haru took Penelope's outstretched wing in his.

They both took flight toward the bats swarming overhead. The egrets decided to join them. The bats now inches from them, made room for them in their group.

Haru pointed to a small spot between a few bats. "Squeeze in here!"

The moonlight shimmered on their wings as they glided through the sky. From here the stars seemed even closer, but still remained well out of reach. The view showed the canopy of the rainforest below.

"Isn't it glorious?" Haru called to them.

Penelope had made good distance ahead of them, but she heard Haru. She replied in her whimsical voice, "Glorious. Glorious. Ru-ruuuuuuuuu!"

"This beats leapin' around on the ground! Woohoo!" Sydney cheered.

Penelope faltered momentarily. Falling out of formation, her wings shuddered in the winds. She continued to spiral down. "Parrot falling. Parrot falling. Time for help!"

A few bats surrounded Penelope. They pulled closer together and gently corralled her back into formation. The egrets were continuing to fly with the bats in their perfect in-sync formation.

Thunder watched the aerial display above. "I wish I could fly."

Soma shuddered in disgust. "I prefer to keep my four feet on the ground, thank you very much."

Thunder's eyes were wide. "But look at them! Wow!! I never knew bats existed. They sure know how to live! It's magical!"

Thunder, being young, had seen very little of the world. The only flying creatures he had really dealt with were the ones that flew during the day. He was not used to nocturnal animals, but he sure was glad he had met some. Wait until he told his herd about Haru and his squadron of bats that lived in the cave near the majestic falls.

Haru swooped low then flew down to the ground near Thunder. His feet swept the ground beneath him trying to gain some sort of leverage, but he crashed on his stomach and his pudgy nose smashed into the ground. When he looked up at them, he had a goofy grin on his face.

The other birds landed next to him with ease. Haru gave

them a thumbs up. "Off to work now! We'll take care of the mosquitoes! It will make your journey easier."

Haru waved good-bye then fluttered off to join the other bats. "Night life! What a life!"

A fruit bat named Lily nodded to Haru as he joined them. "Dinner is served! Oh boy!"

"Any good bugs up here?" asked Haru.

Further from them, Lenny was licking his lips. "The before five buffet! Yay!!"

The three of them circled around the night sky grabbing the mosquitoes in mid-air and gulping them down.

Lester swooped up next to them and almost knocked Lenny out of the way. "Sorry, Lenny."

"No matter." He barely acknowledged the clumsy bat as he continued to fill his belly with tasty treats. "Thwp! Twenty-eight. Thwp! Twenty-nine! Thirty."

Lester heard Lenny's count and his fur perked up on his head. Never one to be beaten, Lester started to vocalize his count. "Mmm! These are delicious! Thwp! Forty-three. Thwp! Forty-four. Thwp! Forty-five!"

Lenny hiccupped. "Uh-oh. I think I ate too fast!"

That was the last Thunder heard from the bats in the sky. They were much farther away now. He smiled up at the moon and continued to wonder at the magic in the night sky. Thunder could not wait to tell his herd about all the things he had seen on his journey home. Maybe if they were lucky, he would find them tomorrow.

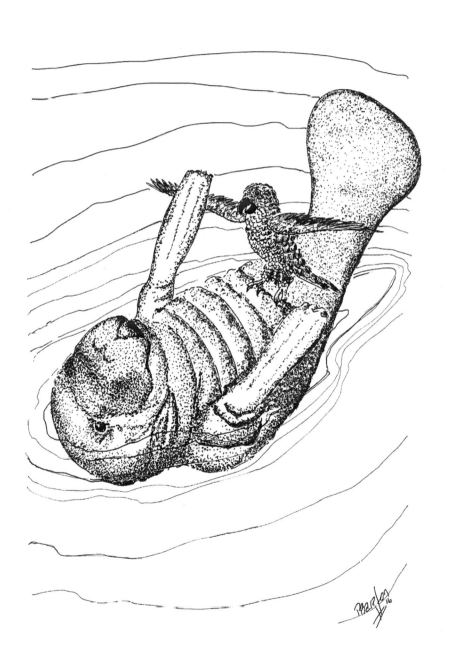

CHAPTER 13
SURFING HIPPOS

Sunlight streamed down from the sky and fell across Thunder's face. He squinted his eyes against the glare. "Just a few more minutes," he murmured. He wrapped his ears around his face in an attempt to shut it out. When that did not work, he stretched his trunk above him in a loud yawn. "Okay. I'm up, I'm up."

Thunder stood up and shook his head. His ears flopped around him as he moved back and forth. Soma was snoring on the ground next to him. "No, no. Not more bats," she grumbled in her sleep.

Thunder giggled at her. He used his trunk to retrieve a small branch from above his sleeping friend and tickled her near her ears. They twitched a few times and two white eyes rolled to glare at him. "What do you want, Thunder?"

"Good morning to you too, Soma. Here's some breakfast." He lowered the branch of berries down to her and stepped back. Turning away, he found his own branches and started to munch away at the red berries.

Penelope stretched on the tree branch above them. "Wake up. Cock-a-doodle-doo." Then the parrot imitated an alarm clock. "Aa-aah-aaah-aah!"

The egrets who were perched near her were grumbling. Cedric snapped a twig from the tree and hurled it at the parrot. It hit her and knocked her out of the tree. She was so caught off guard she landed on her head. Sitting up, she rubbed her wing tip over a small bump that was forming. "Ding! Put a fork in her. Done deal! Rahhh!"

Thunder fell over he was laughing so hard. His front legs covered his belly as loud snuffled laughs flew from his mouth. After the past few days, he had certainly needed that. This realization sobered him. He stood back up, and cleared his throat. "We need to go soon. We're going to find my mom today."

Soma pursed her lips together. "If you say so."

"I do. She's out there, Soma. I know she is." Thunder refused to let negative thoughts take over.

"Right." Soma agreed begrudgingly. She could easily tell the elephant what she thought might have happened, but what right did she have to take his hope away? For her, hope simply did not exist.

"All right. Up and at 'em. I think we should go this way." Thunder pointed his trunk past the cave, where a small worn path. He wasn't sure where it would lead them, but he was ready to start their journey.

"Fine." Soma took one last berry from her branch.

The group traveled in silence. The egrets were seated atop Soma, as usual. Persius was still rubbing sleep from his eyes. Sydney was leaning up against Cedric, her eyes flitted open and closed. Thunder led them up the path that soon went downhill. They traveled slowly down the winding path that was covered with large plants and tall trees that were starting to thin out as they approached the bottom.

A large wall of vines blocked their view. Soma moved over to part them. What they saw before them was so beautiful, they were all shocked. A beach filled with bright white sand was shimmering in the sunlight. Large frothy white waves were breaking over the beach.

"What is that?" Thunder asked, his voice filled with amazement.

"The ocean," answered Soma.

Sydney whistled. "That's something."

"Yeah," agreed Persius.

Penelope landed on Thunder's head and made binoculars over her eyes with her wings. "Ding! Dong! Who's there?"

"Huh?" Thunder squinted his eyes trying to see what Penelope was talking about. "I don't see anything.

A small sound filtered to Thunder's ears. "What is that?" His ears rose next to his head and he tried to take in the sounds that were much farther away. He heard distant music somewhere down the beach. The others looked at him like he had lost his mind, but Thunder did not care. He moved toward the sound of the music.

"Where is he going?" Cedric wondered.

"I don't know, but I think we're about to find out." Soma trailed after him.

Two frogs jumped on top of a large drum that had washed up on the beach. They took turns bouncing up and down creating a beat that was almost catchy.

A large sea turtle lay next to them. He was blowing into a log that had been carved into a long horn. The short puffs accentuated the base the frogs were providing. The light over his back shone over the small ridges that were indented across his blue leathery back.

Four egrets, much like Thunder's own travel companions,

were playing on large peach colored conch shells. The flute-like sounds coming from them were light and carefree. Their feet switched back and forth as they danced along with the music their instruments created.

A long-tailed pangolin was shaking a long stick beside the egrets. His body was covered in small scales that were shaped like tiny artichoke hearts, they continued into his long tail that curled up behind him. His underbelly was covered with dark fur. The stick made a shaking sound, like water falling on a roof top. Every once in a while, he would lick an ant that tried to escape from the top with his long pink tongue.

The closer they got to the group of animals, Thunder could feel the music with every inch of his skin. His tail swished in happy rhythm and his trunk swayed in the air. Even Soma's stern look could not keep him down. His ears waved around him and Thunder danced across the beach to a line of hippos who were dancing joyfully around.

The hippos now circled around him. They were dancing on two legs, with their long skirts fashioned from green grass swaying around them. Large pink flowers were pushed behind their ears. Thunder fell into step behind one of them, as they started a conga line around the beach.

Cedric's eyes were wide as he watched Thunder cutting a rug with the hippos. "Would you look at that?"

"That's not something you see every day," added Persius.

"You can say that again," agreed Sydney.

"What in the world?" Soma was looking at the ocean. A hippo was out in the water and appeared to be surfing on the waves.

The music stopped and the hippos rushed to the water's edge. "Riley!" they cried.

Thunder walked to where the hippos were wading.

"Who's that?"

"Our surf guru, of course," answered the hippo to his left.

Thunder could not help, but wonder what a surf guru was. He moved out of the way, as Riley came sliding onto the beach next to him.

"Hello, little man," Riley greeted him with gusto.

"Hi! I'm Thunder." Thunder was caught up in the happy chaos around him. His herd would never believe it when he told them about the surfing hippos.

"Well, hello, Thunder. I'm Riley. Care to take a turn?" The hippo nodded to the water behind him.

"Can I?" Thunder followed after him. He had never been in the ocean before. His little legs fell out from under him when the first big wave hit his skin. His body toppled over and he landed in a heap on the sandy bottom. When the tide moved back, he gave Soma a goofy grin as he sat there. He ignored her shaking head and turned around to follow Riley into the next wave.

Thunder let his trunk run across the water. The frothy waves tickled him and he giggled. Leaping over small waves of water, he splashed around happily. Jumping in further, he dove all the way in. Swimming out to where Riley was floating, Thunder was happier than he had been in days. He had always loved the water and this water was so easy to float in.

Thunder surfed the first wave with Riley and was surprised at how quickly the wave's momentum pushed his body through the water. He had already swum back and was ready to catch another wave when he saw a dark shadow beneath him. A big animal was sleeping soundly beneath the surface, with two rounded flippers crossed over its belly. It caught Thunder so off guard that he tumbled when the wave pushed him into the surf.

"What was that?"

"What?"

"That!" Thunder pointed at the dark shape in the water with his trunk.

Penelope called from above, "Shark attack! Big teeth! Chomp, chomp!"

Riley shook his head at the silly bird. "That's no shark. That's Manny."

"What's a Manny?" Thunder looked at him in confusion.

"Not what, who, little man. Follow along now. That's my buddy Manny. He's a manatee."

"Manny Manatee." Penelope repeated in her singsong voice.

At that moment, Manny chose to surface in the water. "Good morning, Riley." His voice was deep and rough from sleep.

"Daylight's a wastin', Manny. About time you showed your mug up here. Waves are crashing, man." Riley gestured to the water around them.

"Gnarly." Manny turned over on his back and let the waves wash over his belly. He continued to ride the wave further down to the beach. When he got there, he flipped over and dove deeper into the water.

Thunder scanned the area around him, wondering where the large manatee had gone to. When he saw a dark shape moving slowly toward him, this time he did not panic. "Look! There he is!"

Manny rose up and spouted water from his pudgy lips. It landed right between Thunder's eyes. "Bullseye!"

"Hey!" Thunder turned to him and shook his trunk. "This is war!"

Thunder sucked up the salty water into his trunk and blasted Manny with full force. The manatee stretched his neck and let the water fall all over him. "Oh yea! Right there." He shrugged his shoulders as if he were satisfying an itch.

"You're silly!" Thunder giggled at him.

"Silly's a state of mind, my friend. A happy state." Manny turned and saw a large wave breaking in the distance and a floating mountain. He pointed it out to Thunder. "Disgustin'"

As soon as Manny pointed out the floating mountain, Thunder heard a sound as loud as ten elephants trumpeting together. He saw uprights throw things from the mountain into the water. "Wow, what is that?"

"The uprights toss things they don't want into our waters," Manny said. "Some of it washes up on our shores, and some of it makes us sick."

"Wow, that's not good," Thunder said sadly.

"You are so right, my friend." Manny rolled over and let his belly face the sun. He caught Penelope's attention from above.

She squawked, "Catch a wave! Surf's up."

Penelope dove down to the manatee and landed on his belly. She lifted her wings up and bobbed her head from side to side as she maintained her balance. "Hang ten! Cowabunga!"

Thunder watched his friend and smiled. "Wow, Penelope. You're good!"

Penelope leapt off of the manatee before the ocean waves crashed over him. She still managed to get soaked in the process. Tumbling through the air, she landed on the beach with a thud. Shaking the water out of her ears, she quipped, "Land ahoy! No place like home. Rahhhh!"

Thunder and Riley both exited the water behind her. Manny stayed in the water. "Time for some breakfast. I'll check you later, Riley."

"I think you mean lunch, Manny, but yeah, I'll see you later, dude." Riley shook his head at the departing manatee. Turning to Thunder he said, "So little man, what brings you here to my little paradise?

This was the first time the hippo was really addressing him and Thunder felt the eyes of all the hippos turn to him. "I'm looking for my mother."

"Your mother?" Riley looked at him with concern. "Did she swim off, bruh?"

"No. The uprights came and captured our herd. I got away and I've been trying to find her ever since. My friends are helping."

Riley shook his head. "That's a sad story indeed. That reminds me of another one."

Soma snorted near them. "Great. Here we go."

"Have you ever heard of the Great Tusker in the sky?"

Thunder looked at Riley in confusion. "No."

"Oh, you have much to learn, little man. There is an elephant in the sky who watches over us all. He is the Great Tusker. For centuries the Great Tusker watched as man and animal lived side by side. There was a balance among them, but man grew apart from the land. He became greedy, wanting to build up a world that was separate from the wild. In doing so, he interrupted the great balance. Man took from the earth, from the bounty of the land and treasures from our kind. He became obsessed with material possessions."

Thunder was paying close attention to what he said. "That's horrible."

"It is, but the legend says that man can walk with the beast again. He just needs to be reminded of the way things used to be. When he does, the Great Tusker will smile down

95

on us again."

"Wow. That's a stretch," Soma muttered. "Great Tusker, bah! I'll believe that when I see it." The egrets on her back were nodding their heads in agreement.

"Oh, quiet you!" Thunder shushed her. He was still young enough that he believed that magic could exist.

"Don't worry, little man. He does exist." Riley's eyes twinkled in the sunlight.

"I hope I get to see him someday."

"You may at that," answered Riley.

"Thunder, we should keep moving if you want to find your mother." Soma interjected into the moment.

"Right." Thunder knew Soma was right. He should not have spent his morning on such foolish antics, but he just couldn't help it. "Thank you for the story, Riley. We do need to go."

Thunder and the rest of the group started to make their way across the beach, when Riley called across to them. "Wait, little man. I saw a farm not far from here where there were many uprights. If the uprights took them, you might find them there."

A huge smile broke across Thunder's face. "Really? Oh, thank you!"

"You're welcome." Riley turned away from them and led the other hippos into the ocean to continue their morning surf lessons.

"You heard him. Let's go find that farm!" Thunder led the others down the beach. His head was filled with hope that would never fade. With a lighter step, he did not even let Soma's grumpy face kill his joy as they continued to move on.

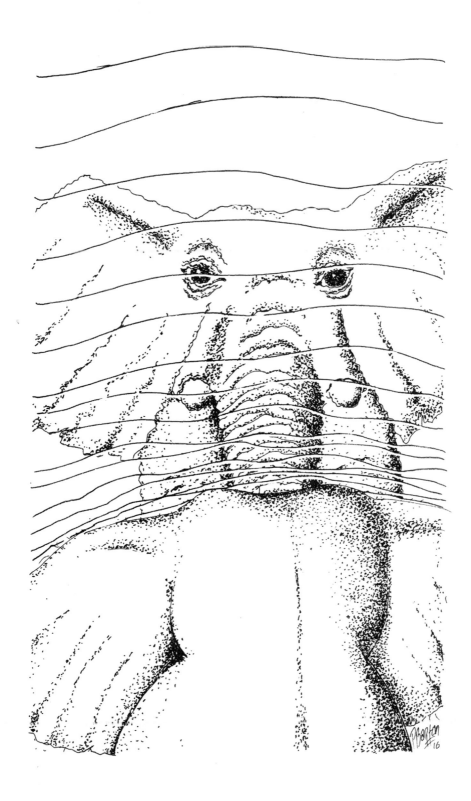

CHAPTER 14
A NEW LOOK FOR THUNDER

In the morning light, the jungle was alive with noises. The birds chirped from above, the monkeys were howling playfully in the trees, and a green tree frog croaked on the forest floor before jumping into the pond for a swim, as Thunder and Soma walked past the waterfall. The egrets were resting on Soma's back. Penelope had chosen a perch on Thunder's head.

Thunder looked at the frog within the water and walked closer to the edge. Penelope jumped off Thunder and flew onto a branch overhanging the pond as Thunder lowered his head to watch the frog skirt across the water's surface.

Soma stopped at the berry bush and gobbled them up. Her jaw gnashed together and the juice from the berries ran down her face. "Delicious."

Cedric spotted Thunder about to fill his trunk like a long watering hose and squeaked. "Oh no! Not again! Didn't you just have a bath?"

"Just when we thought we were on our way to paradise." Persius lamented.

Thunder sucked up a trunk full of water and let it spray

into the air over his back. Penelope got splashed in the process. Her feathers were now sticking up in disarray. "All wet. All wet." She made a strangling gurgle sound. "Eek!"

Thunder giggled. "Sorry, Penelope."

"Towel?" Penelope squawked. "Towel?"

Thunder snickered. "How about a blow dry, Penny?"

The parrot tightened her grip on the low hanging branch in preparation. Thunder blew hot air from his trunk and started to dry her feathers.

"Penelope. Penelope. Not a coin. No copper. Feathers flying." She tilted her head at him.

"Sorry, Penelope. What was I thinking?" Thunder replied.

"Ding dong! Doorbell. No one's home. Elephant dryer." She squawked aloud and chirped like a baby bird.

Thunder giggled at the parrot. He still had trouble understanding the bird from time to time. "Okay, okay, Penelope. Whatever you say."

Thunder peered down into the water and noticed small tusks starting to bud on his face. "Oh no, I've changed. Look!"

Penelope's gold eyes flashed red in excitement. She seemed to understand the implications of the ivory starting to grow on her friend. "Tusks for trinkets. Tusks for trinkets. Eek! Watch out!"

Soma shook her head solemnly. "The end of innocence."

Thunder gasped. "Oh no! Does that make me a target now?"

Soma tried to console him. "Look on the bright side. With big tusks, you can spear anyone who comes too close."

"I don't want to do that!" His ears flapped anxiously behind him. Thunder touched his new tusks with his trunk, wondering how they had come so close to the surface overnight. Maybe this place was magical.

99

"A new look. Uh-oh, uh-oh," quipped Penelope.

"Uh-oh is right, Penelope. Now I really have to hide. I better get back to my herd soon."

Penelope flew up to a tall mahogany then strolled across a high branch. She could hear a buzzing sound that reminded her of a swarm of locusts. It was the sound of vuvuzuelas being blown by the uprights. She had heard that sound before.

Thunder perked his ears up then splayed them out wide. He strained forward to listen. "What is that sound?"

"Nothing. Forget it." Soma too was familiar with that sound. Uprights. This was not the time to look for any kind of danger with them. She lumbered over to a burned out tree trunk and sharpened the jagged edges of her horn on the bark.

Penelope trained her ears on the loud noise. "Playing music. Not Mozart." She whistled in disappointment.

"Go scout for us, Penelope." Thunder suggested.

Penelope flew off and soared above the forest canopy toward the village. In the distance she could see villagers that were banging on pots and pans. Some were blowing into the long horned vuvuzuelas that made the humming sound. They were purposely making loud noises.

The parrot watched as a herd of elephants were startled by the ruckus. Some ran wild away from the frightening noises. Two elephants ran into a Jeep and tipped it over sideways in their dash to get away. A few others bumped into huts, breaking pieces off the walls and pulling down portions of the roofs. One elephant stepped on Mosi's bicycle before tearing through a clothesline near it. The rope remained attached to him and clothes fluttered in the wind around him as he raced away from the scene.

People were screaming and scattering in all directions. They tried to avoid the charging elephants as they scrambled past them.

Panicked, the elephants made a beeline past the shacks and out through the electric fences that had been put up in hopes that it would keep them out. The elephants ran toward open land with sparks flying all around them. The sharp biting pain of the electricity did nothing more than shock them. They continued their mad scrambling.

Penelope's eyes widened as she soared through the air. She said to herself, "Back to their rooms. Back home. Tirrred. Tirrred."

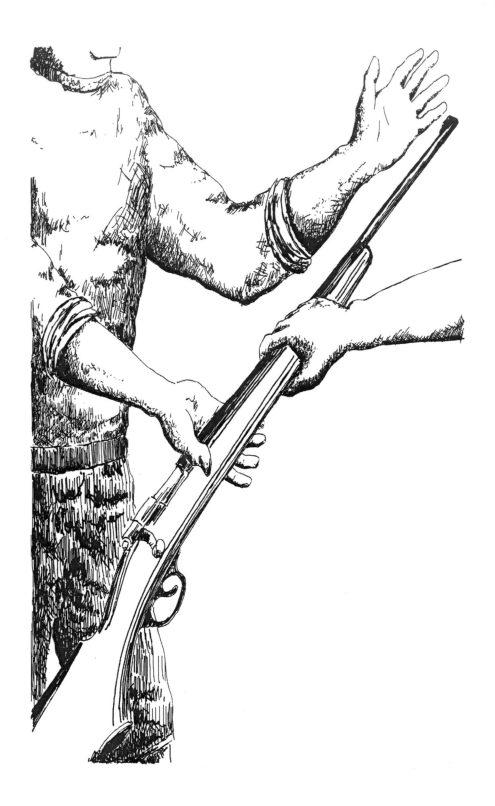

CHAPTER 15
FAMILY FIRST

Mosi and other terrified, angry residents surveyed the damage to their village. The massive elephant stampede had torn apart their homes.

Mosi shook his head in anguish. "Look! Look! Look what they've done! All our hard work! Gone!"

"I've done everything right and look where it's gotten me!" He eyed the downed electrical wires wondering what he was supposed to do now. He believed in the balance of man and animal. Mosi always had, but nothing he tried had worked. All the laws of the land went out the window now. He had a family to take care of.

The other villagers started to chime in. An older man near him shouted, "Time to get our crops back!"

"Yeah!!" agreed another, then another woman shouted, "Yes!!"

Mosi could see the villagers would be out for blood soon. It hurt his heart to see them this way, but he had to admit he was at his limit. There was only so much a man could take. He shook his head in disbelief at the remnants of the peaceful village that had always felt so much like home. He picked up his bicycle, and walked away with the bent front wheel squeaking as it turned.

He turned over options in his head, but none of them had a pleasant consequence. Life was filled with difficult choices, but loving his family was the easiest one. He had to put them first.

Penelope shook the images from her mind. She flew back to where her friends were waiting for her report. She landed on the rock next to them. "Danger lurks! Danger. Graugh!"

Soma sniffed irritably. "Tell me something new."

Thunder lowered his head so his eyes were closer to the parrot's golden orbs. "What was it, Penelope?"

"Uprights. Don't scare the elephants." Penelope made a whirring siren sound. "Ah—ooooo-oooo-oooo."

Thunder's ears perked up. "Elephants? They're alive?! I wanna see!"

Soma cautioned Thunder, "Not so fast."

"But what if it's them? My herd! I have to know! My mom…" Thunder bolted ahead of them, not sticking around to see if Soma approved. Penelope and the egrets flew through the air to keep an eye on him.

Soma sauntered after him shaking her head. "Kids! When will they learn?"

Penelope flew overhead. "Let's go fly. Wheeeeee!!"

Thunder ran as fast as he could. The ground shook beneath his feet. When he got closer to a wire fence, he slammed on the brakes. Peering across the way he saw elephants grazing far off across what looked like acres of farmland. He had never seen elephants so close to where the uprights lived before. His herd had always stayed close to the watering hole near the rainforest.

He did not understand what he was seeing. "Huh? Home?" In his mind, wherever the herd had been was where he was supposed to be.

Penelope landed on Thunder. Soma stopped a few paces behind Thunder with the egrets hovering above her head.

The egrets caught up and stopped short. No one said a word.

Thunder gathered himself up and leaned forward. "Okay, time to focus. Just like Mom used to say." He rumbled and stomped his feet the way he had been taught. He did what he could to communicate to the herd. "I hope they hear me! Please hear me! Please! Please!"

When no one responded, Thunder's ears fell against his head. Sometimes it took time to get a response, but this was longer than usual. What if they could not hear him anymore? He sat down on the ground and smacked the ground with his trunk in disappointment.

Thunder remembered snatches of moments in his head. The friendly herd who had rumbled back and forth with them, splashing in the watering hole with his friends, and most of all the loving hugs from his adoring mom. Would he ever see her again?

In the village marketplace, Drago crept closer to the dark building near the outskirts of town. He turned to make sure no one else was watching him. Knocking quietly, he opened the door which creaked loudly in protest. He looked at the men sitting at the table surrounded by a cloud of smoke.

One of them nodded at him to come closer. "What do you have, Drago?" he asked with a cigar stuck in the corner of his mouth.

"More elephants, boss." He stepped closer and stood for the boss man to inspect him.

"How many?"

"An entire herd."

"Eh? Well then. Half now, the other when you bring me what I need." The boss man handed him a stack of money and Drago quickly retrieved it. "Make sure to bring them back this time, yes?"

Drago gulped loudly. "Yes, boss." He turned away from the table and closed his eyes imagining all the things he would buy when the elephants were harvested of their ivory. He counted the stack of bills as he exited the building. Checking to make sure no one saw him leave, Drago stashed the money deep into the pockets of his pants.

Turning back to the village marketplace Drago saw Mosi and approached him. "Hey, Mosi. You could get rid of them, you know. Permanently. I can help you, cousin."

Mosi shook his head. "I don't want to hurt them, Drago. I just want them to go away!"

Drago chuckled at Mosi, champion of the beasts. "Aahh… but do you know how much money you can make? It's a lot more now. Tusks and horns can get you a handsome sum! No more worries ever again!"

Mosi had finally had enough. "Tchah! Give me your gun, then!"

"That's it, cousin! Finally thinking right." Drago retrieved a rifle from his pickup and handed it to Mosi.

Mosi did a double take. "What? Drago, you got another new truck? How can you afford such a luxury?

Drago snickered. "Ha! Life is sweet now, cousin. You'll have all the best soon enough, ya?"

Mosi grabbed the rifle from Drago and jumped on his wobbly bicycle. "Don't wait for me!" Mosi pedaled off down the road as storm clouds formed overhead. Today, he would find a way to solve all his family's problems.

CAUTION

ELECTRIFIED
FENCE !!

CHAPTER 16
HOT WIRE

Thunder stared across the field again. The elephant herd was slowly lumbering off out of sight. Panic rose in his chest. How was he going to find his herd, if they kept moving? "They're going away!"

Penelope shook her head sadly. "Nobody's home. Ring the doorbell."

"There's no doorbell, you pedantic parrot!" Sydney corrected her.

Penelope shook her head at Sydney and mimicked the sound of a doorbell. "Ding! Dong! Ding, dong, ding!"

Sydney slanted her head at the parrot. "Ha, ha, ha. Very funny." The sarcasm was only lost on Penelope.

Thunder continued to look off in the distance. "Penelope, can you take a closer look?"

"Aye, aye, captain." She raised her gray wings and nodded to Thunder before taking off into the air. When she got closer to the fields, she circled around it once then returned back.

"Moat. Castle bound. Raise the battlements." Penelope said as she landed on a branch nearby.

"Great. More obstacles," grumbled Soma.

Thunder's eyes were fearful again. "Oh no. Not again." Nothing seemed to be going their way.

"Demons are at the gate." Soma shook her head.

Persius patted the rhino consolingly. "We'll figure it out."

Sydney glared at Persius. "No pressure."

Cedric agreed with Sydney. "That's not something I want to cross."

Penelope shook her head sadly. "Can't go there. Door closed. Not today. Not for the four-leggeds."

"Yeah, but not for us!" Sydney interrupted the gloom.

Cedric put his wingtip on his beak and shushed, "Shhh!! We're in this together! It's no good if we don't all get across!"

"Unsafe territory. No, no, no." Penelope made clicking sounds with her tongue on the roof of her mouth.

Cedric pointed up to a circuit box. "Look!"

The egrets jumped back in fright when they saw where Cedric was gesturing. Persius almost tumbled from Soma's back, but Sydney helped to steady him.

"Eek!! It's a hot wire." Sydney shrieked.

Persius put his wings behind his back and squared his eyes on the box. "We have to turn the power off! Are you ready?"

"No! Not really," Sydney said in a panic. "Let's say we did and come back another day, huh?"

Persius shook his head. "Great! I never thought of you as a scaredy-cat, Sydney. It's plum embarrison'."

Sydney puffed out her chest and ruffled her feathers. "I'm not a scaredy-cat!"

Persius's beak turned up in a grin. "Allrightythen! Let's go flip that switch!"

Sydney's eyes bugged, but she kept her beak shut this time.

The egrets darted up and over the circuit box. Circling around it, they took turns pecking at it with their dagger like beaks. They aimed for the wire terminals with each strike.

A zap of light burst from the wire shocking Sydney enough to make her feathers singe. "Oops! Ow! Ow! Ow!"

She stiffened in the air, and fell like a bomb heading toward the ground. She opened her wings before she landed hard on the ground where she lay unconscious.

Persius cautioned, "Don't touch that one! It's a live wire!"

Cedric tilted his head. "Too late."

Sydney woke up and shook her feathers out. She walked around unsteady for a few steps, teetering first to the right then the left. "Oh, I knew I didn't want to do this. Now just see where it got me. Where am I? Is it hot in here or what?"

Sydney walked a few more steps then fell back down. The other two egrets swooped down to help her up.

"Look! Over there!" Thunder pointed with his trunk to where a few uprights were bent over weeding their garden with hoes. He took a few steps in that direction, but Soma moved in front of him and blocked his path.

"Don't go there, Thunder," she warned.

Penelope gave a sharp shrill whistle. "No, thank you."

"That's right. That's not gonna fly," agreed Soma.

"Are you trying to be funny?" Sydney glanced up at Soma.

Persius blinked his eyes in confusion. "What? What was so funny? What did I miss? Soma was funny? Somebody please tell me!"

Sydney snorted through her beak. "Never mind. Aaakk! Never mind."

Thunder tried to push Soma away. "But what if it's them? What if they got away?"

Penelope addressed Thunder, "Hello, honey. Glad you're

back."

"Yeah! And the good news is no one's after us," interjected Cedric.

Sydney hooted, "Bingo! We're in the clear! Smooth sailing! Let's go!"

Soma shook her head at them. "That's what you think."

A bug flew near the electric fence. It caught Sydney's eyes. She was about to hop after it when it flew directly into the fence. A loud sizzle was followed by a burning smell that made the others jump back.

"What to do? What to do?" Penelope's head hovered on her neck from left to right. "Can't go there."

Thunder stomped his feet again and the ground trembled beneath his feet. His ears perked up around his face and he listened in desperation. He stomped again, so hard that the dust kicked up around them making Sydney cough. He watched in helplessness as the herd started to disappear from sight.

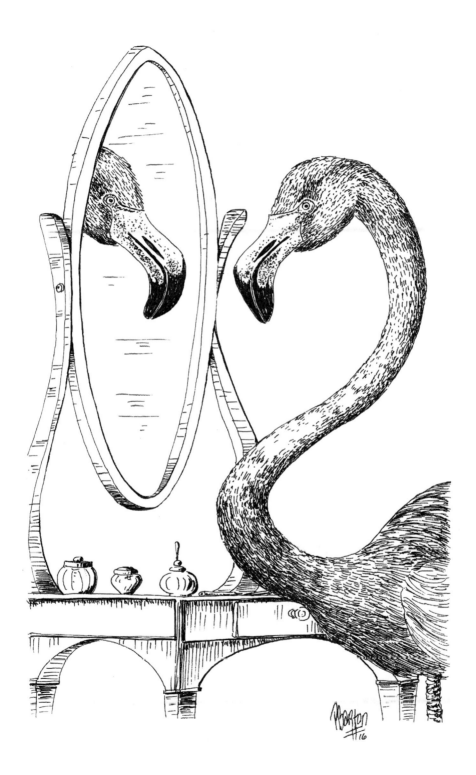

CHAPTER 17
FREDERICK

Thunder sat down on the ground and thumped it with his trunk. More dust flew around them. Waving his ears, he fanned the dust away from his face. It billowed out in small little puffs of dirt that covered Sydney's white coat.

"Hey! What are you doin', kid? Sending smoke signals?" Sydney asked him.

"Noooo! I'm trying to...oh never mind."

Just then, a shadow passed over them. The group looked up to see some kind of pink blur zooming past them. Penelope leapt under Thunder's legs and hid. They both crouched closer the ground to duck from the bird's dramatic flyovers.

The pink mass above them dived down and swooped low over their heads. The egrets ducked beneath Soma, not quite sure what was headed their way. Frederick, the pink flamingo, was clearly amused by his own antics. His loud cackling laugh could be heard as he flew back and started to make another pass at them.

Thunder peered up at the flamingo and then his eyes grew wide when he saw the flamingo was about to come back. "Duck!"

114

"Duck, duck, goose!" squawked Penelope.

Frederick put both his wings in front of him as he dived, pretending to be some kind of fighter jet. He made machine gun noises from his beak. "Rat-a-tat-tat-tat!"

Soma charged at the intruder, but could not make contact with him. The egrets fell off her back and tumbled to the ground in a flurry of feathers and dust.

Frederick gave a dramatic sigh and turned away from them. He landed a few yards ahead of them, next to a small lagoon. Thunder heard him speaking to himself from here, but could not make out his words. He shook his head and decided to find out what he was up to. The others followed him. Penelope flew above them and landed on a rock near him.

"Well, hello, gorgeous!" Frederick had picked up a small handheld mirror and was staring at his reflection. He was standing next to a small dresser that had several garments hanging out from crooked drawers that seemed mismatched. A small vanity table was in front of him. A make-shift dressing room was hidden between two large boulders. Thunder could only guess that the flamingo had created this area for himself.

Penelope strutted over to Frederick and waited for him to notice her. She primped and preened her feathers, mimicking the flamingo's motions. The flamingo was so obsessed that he had no clue the parrot was anywhere near him. He put his mirror down for a minute.

"Now where's my makeup?" Frederick checked all over his body to make sure that no feather was out of place. He made a kissing motion at himself in his mirror. "Ooh-la-la!"

Penelope bobbed up and down on the rock, another desperate attempt to get his attention. The egrets flew down next to her and were eyeing her like she had completely lost what was left of her loopy mind.

Penelope became impatient and interrupted the flamboyant flamingo. "What's your name? What's your name?"

A haughty laugh broke free from his mouth. "I heard you the first time! Ah, ha, ha, ha, ha, ha!!!" Grabbing the mirror off the vanity table again, Frederick inspected his face once more.

"Name, name, name. What's in a name?" Penelope continued.

"Well, if you must know, I am Frederick! With a k." Frederick gestured to himself with a few dramatic flourishes of his wing. "Can't you see I'm preoccupied?"

He paused briefly before continuing, "You know, we flamingos don't like to be alone...and I have a big date tonight. I have to look, well, you know, mahvelous, dahling!"

Sydney let out a low whistle. "Now where would a fine bird such as yourself find all this stuff?"

Frederick brushed off her comment with a wave of his wing. "It's amazing what the uprights discard these days. They have no regard for the mess they leave behind either. One upright's trash is another bird's treasure, I always say. And it all looks mahvelous here, doesn't it?"

Frederick stopped his primping for a moment. He turned to Penelope and gave her a once over. "And just who are you?"

Penelope jumped up on Frederick's vanity table and cocked her head. She was entranced with the bird in the mirror. "A mirror. Where's Penelope?"

Her beak tapped the mirror a few times. "Peekaboo!" Tilting her head, she gave a whistle. "Ru-roooo. There you are!"

Penelope tapped the mirror. "I'm Penelope."

Thunder, Soma, and the egrets move in closer to Penelope.

By now, the flamingo was clearly no threat. Thunder looked at him curiously. "Are you a flamingo dancer?"

Frederick gasped and put his hand to his chest in mock disgust. "Honey, do I look like a *flamenco* dancer? What do you think I am? A hair piece? A chicken dinner?" He shook his head and continued, "An objet d'art? Really! Can't you appreciate real beauty when you see it?"

Frederick looked down and gasped. He picked something from his plumage and turned around to wag his wing tip at Soma. "And you with the Mack truck torso..."

Soma lowered her horn at him. "Grrrrrr!"

He put his wing on her horn and shushed her away. "Don't you be trying to poke me with that weapon there. Not in my house, girlfriend! Weapons at the door please." Frederick stared Soma in the eye and cocked his head at her. His spindly legs were just as precocious in their posture.

Soma reared back on her haunches and prepared to charge at the flashy bird. Persius grabbed on for dear life onto anything his wings could grip. "Uh-oh! Don't make her mad."

"Yeah, bad things'll happen!" Cedric warned as Soma put her feet back down.

"What-e-v-e-r!" Frederick let his head wiggle as his snapped his wing tips together in a feisty circle.

Penelope chose that moment to interrupt. "Elephants, trunks, tails. Seen any?"

"Not in this neighborhood, Miss Thing! Tsk! Tsk!" His eyelashes fluttered for a moment as he really took in the parrot in front of him. "Nice coloring. Who does your feathers?"

Penelope squawked and flapped her wings. "Feathers are fine." She whistled at him and waited for him to redirect his attention to something more serious. "Help Thunder. Time to go home."

Soma sighed. "Here we go. I doubt he can help us after all."

"Try me, sister," the flamingo challenged her.

Soma huffed at him. She would be married before she would ever consider be related to this foolish creature. "He lost his herd."

"Right." Frederick turned back to the mirror and took a stick from the table. He dipped it in a dark black mud, which he painted around the outside of his eyelids making his eyes look even more dramatic. He dipped his wing into some crushed berries and started to use them on the tips of his feathers at the top of his head. This made the pink seem even brighter with the dark reds accentuating the top.

The egrets flew up and landed on the mirror above the table. "Yeah, gone! Split! Disappeared!" Cedric shook the mirror with his feet to express his point.

Sydney added, "Vanished! Poof!"

"Without a trace!" Persius expressed.

Sydney whispered down to Frederick, "I think they're..." She cleared her throat. "Well, you know..."

Cedric interrupted her. "And we have to find them. But... ha hum...in the meantime, we need to get to the other side. I mean, the other side of that large field over there." He pointed with his wing. "Where the elephants are."

"And not be seen," interrupted Persius.

"Yeah, to my herd!" Thunder chimed in.

Soma shook her head sadly. "He thinks he's gonna find home."

"Home? Oh, child, you've come to the right place. Look!" Frederick waved his wings and scanned the largess of his impressive digs. He gestured to the space around him.

He was sitting at the plush chair in front the vanity mirror that was attached to a table. To his right was a sitting room with a large exotic area rug lining the floor. There were a few wicker chairs with plush purple velvet pillows covering them. A velvet lined sofa was in between those chairs. Next to that was a curtain of vines covered with glass beads that shimmered in the sunlight as they casted colorful rainbows around them. Frederick's nest sat behind the curtain. The nest was made of many colorful sheets that had been shredded into strips that were easily woven into a cozy little bed for him.

"You don't take too life seriously, do you?" asked Soma.

Frederick relaxed at his vanity table and used his dainty feathers to pick up a hairbrush. Sliding it through his feathers, the flamingo answered her. "Well, life is short. What else can a beauty like me do? Hmmm?"

Penelope made a wolf whistle. "Ru-ruuuuuuu. Yum, yum, yum, yum, yum!"

Frederick stuck out his legs and began to check his toe nails. He ignored the others as he did so.

Soma found the flamingo's attention span less than satisfying. Her hoof pounded the ground. "Where are the uprights?"

Frederick turned to face her. "Well! Let me tell you. Those uprights! No fashion sense whatsoever!" He waved his wing in the air.

"Oh!"

Penelope waved her wing over her beak. "Phew. Phew."

Frederick gestured for Thunder to come closer. "Come over here, Mr. Thunder. Let me look at those nails. When's the last time you had a pedicure? My, oh my. How about some pink polish for those paws?"

Thunder growled at him. "They're not paws!"

Cedric jumped down on the table before the vanity. "We need your help!"

Penelope paced on the rock below. "Making him mad. Making him mad."

"Oy! Don't get your feathers in a tizzy! You came to the right place. Just give me a minute. Let me think. Hm." Frederick sashayed over to the dresser and opened a cabinet door.

"Don't you worry about those uprights. I haven't seen any lately. Why do you think I'm still here? Hmmm?" Frederick continued. He turned to Thunder. "Now you just park yourself in front of my new vanity mirror...and look! You can see yourself in it!"

Frederick shuffled through clothes on hangers.

"Aahh ha ha ha ha ha!! And when I'm done with you, you'll be so pretty, like me, my sweet young thing...and..."

Thunder's blood was boiling. "Gahhhh!"

Frederick ignored him. His voice was high pitched with excitement. "And life will be sweet and light."

The flamingo waltzed over to him, swinging a long, colorful scarf around Thunder. "And you'll love all sentient beings. Karma will be your friend and calmness will be your essence. Shall we proceed? Hmmmm?" Frederick batted his eyelashes again at Thunder and up at Penelope.

Thunder turned from the flamingo and leaned over the lagoon. Soma pulled leaves off a bush and munched. The egrets rested on her back as silence fell over them.

Cedric shook his head. "Oh, brother. Here we go."

"Yeah, the show's started!" Sydney chimed in.

Penelope shook her head from side to side on the rock as she lifted one foot after the other. "Yum, yum, yum. Home for dinner."

120

"It's gonna be a long afternoon. Aye!" Cedric mumbled. He knew what Thunder was going to do next.

Thunder waded into the pond and filled his trunk with water. He sprayed out in all directions attempting to be playful. It helped him think when his mind was too full and this flamingo had certainly been filling it up with nonsense.

"Here's some for you, Soma!" Thunder aimed his trunk towards Soma and drenched her.

Soma let her shoulders relax under the water. "Aaahhh."

The egrets tried to jump off Soma's back, but still managed to get drenched in the deluge of water.

"Yikes!" shouted Cedric.

Sydney complained with a shriek, "Hey!"

Persius huffed from his beak. "Stop that! I already had my shower today!"

Sydney blew the water from her face. "Pft! Pft!"

Persius grumbled at Thunder. "You could have at least warned us!"

Thunder burst out laughing. The egrets plopped back down to the ground, soaked. They were clearly unhappy.

Cedric eyed him angrily. "Yeah! What do you think this is? A water park?"

Sydney tilted her head at Cedric. "What's that?"

"Never mind," said Cedric.

Sydney stuck her beak in the air. "Pft!"

"Where's a towel when you need one?" Persius lamented.

Sydney pointed toward Frederick. "I bet he has one! Or two or three or…"

The birds shook their heads at Sydney, each one refusing to go talk to the eccentric flamingo who was now back to powdering his face in front of his mirror. They stretched their wings out and let the sun dry them as Thunder continued to frolic in the water.

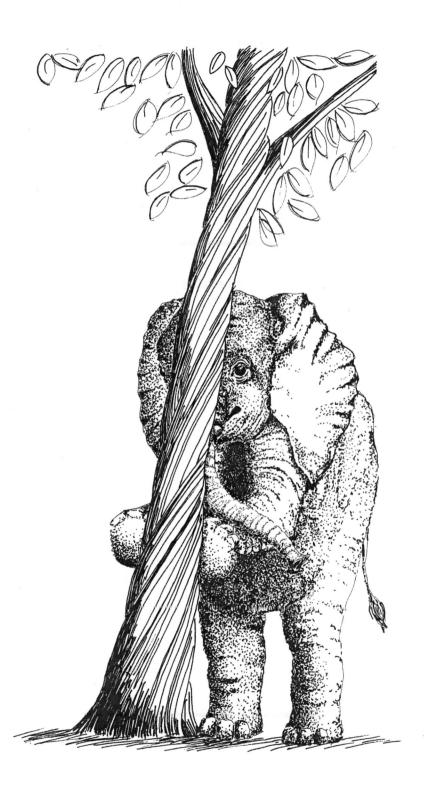

CHAPTER 18
UNICORNS

Frederick flew down next to the lagoon and gazed inside. The water rippled with Thunder's frolicking and his reflection turned blurry before him. "Aaahhh! My face! What happened? Oh no! Wrinkles!!"

Flapping his wings around him in a panic, he put one to his chest and held on, as if his heart were about to explode. "Everything was fine a minute ago! Oh! Oh! My face!! Where's my night cream?"

Frederick turned to Thunder, snapped his wing tips together, and pointed to his vanity table. "Quick! Hand me that jar!"

Thunder reached around the boulder with his trunk. He wrapped it around the jar, picked it up from the table, and stretched so that his trunk brought it toward Frederick.

The flustered flamingo grabbed the jar quickly from him and opened it up. The ripples faded in the water before him. Frederick peered into the lagoon and saw his reflection again. "Oh, wait! Who's that? Oh, it's me! I've come back! Oh! What a relief!"

Frederick let out a nervous laugh, relaxing slightly, then

feigned as if he were going to faint. "Oh my! I was beginning to feel like a cat on a hot tin roof! Bring me my wine, Scarlet! Where's my handkerchief? Oh, oh!"

Soma rolled her eyes from the mud nearby. "Here we go again."

Frederick walked over to the vanity table, plucked a tissue from the box, and turned to Penelope. "Did you see that movie?"

Penelope whistled at him. "Frederick is a flamingo."

Frederick wiped his brow in confusion. "What?"

Penelope titled her head at him as he looked in the mirror. "Nice to see you."

Frederick shook his head at her. "Nice to see you? I don't even know you! You're losin' your feathers, girlfriend."

Penelope squawked. "Ick! Ick! Ick!"

The flamingo muttered to himself, "I traded a nice comfortable life in a high-rise for this? What was I thinking?"

Thunder walked from the pond and stopped closer to Frederick. He leaned forward and froze, and his ears jutted out around his head. He listened with his feet as the ground moved beneath it.

Penelope cocked her head at him with a puzzled look plastered over her face. "What-a-ya doin'? What-a-ya doin'?"

"Sending a message and trying to hear the earth move," Thunder answered her.

"Move the earth?" Penelope stomped her feet on the tree branch above him.

"Yes, elephants can do that. Didn't you know?" Thunder replied.

Frederick ignored the pair of them and continued to preen himself. He was fixated on getting his feathers styled just right.

Penelope jumped down from the tree branch and paced back and forth on the ground in front of Thunder. Penelope nodded to Thunder with her beak. "Thunder's an elephant. Big feet. Soft soles. Can move the earth. Woooooo."

"Yes. And I bet they are back in the field. We have to get back to them, before they leave again!"

Frederick put a wing up and gestured to them. "Yoo-hoo? I'll be right there!" He sashayed over to Thunder and Penelope. He noticed Soma in the mud. "Girlfriend, you got the right idea!"

Soma rolled over and grumbled to herself. She had better things to do than listen to the foolish flamingo.

Frederick turned back to Thunder and propped his wing under his chin in contemplation. "I'm here! Now, where's my pupil? Ah, there he is. Are you ready to learn some style?"

Frederick sashayed in front of them, showing off his fancy walk. "Some grace?" He posed one wing above his head, and one wrapped around his stomach. "And some poise?"

The flamingo made another shape in front of them. "Ah, ha, ha, ha, ha, ha!"

He grabbed Thunder's trunk with his wing tips and talked into it like it was a microphone. "Are you paying attention?"

Thunder replied nasally, "I'm here! Front and center!"

"And you with the mud pack, spa time is over! Come out and join the party!"

Soma trudged out of the mud hole. The egrets flew over and resettled onto her back.

Frederick gestured to all of them. "Now listen! You can't just traipse over that big open field and think the uprights are not going to see you. Oh no, honey. They'll sound the alarm and end your life as you know it!"

"I thought you didn't know anything about the uprights?"

Soma asked him.

"Well, of course I do, but they bore me, dahling. Nothing flashy about those uprights over there. Nothing to see there, honey. And I like my hide where it is just fine. I wouldn't want to be turned into some exotic head piece after all. Although I'm sure I would make any upright look fashion forward with my feathers."

"Right," muttered Soma.

"You have to follow my lead," assuaged Frederick.

"Okay? So now what?" asked Thunder.

Frederick answered, still stuck on his last train of thought. "Yes, honey pie, they will end you." He paused for emphasis. "Now watch me. I'll show you the art of hiding in the forest. You have to become one with the trees—if you know what I mean."

Frederick pranced over to a tree and disappeared behind it. "You have to think like a tree."

The funny flamingo contorted his body to match the tall thin shape of the tree. Not a single feather could be seen behind the trunk. "Just like this!"

Frederick returned from behind the tree ignoring the puzzled looks that Thunder and Soma shared. "Now it's your turn."

Thunder walked behind the tree, but his round body stuck out on both sides. He stood up on his tippytoes, and let his legs stretch over his head. The tree shook under his weight, its leaves rattling loudly in protest.

Soma moved behind the tree next to him. She sucked in a deep breath to get skinnier. She almost pulled it off, but her horn stuck out from behind the tree.

"How's this Frederick?" called Thunder.

Frederick put his wing over his head and shook his head.

127

"No, no, no. That won't work."

The egrets broke out in a fit of giggles.

Soma was struggling behind the tree. Her face was turning different shades of purple and red. She let out a huge exhale that sent a gust of air past Frederick and the egrets. Their feathers were all pointing sideways from the rush of wind.

Frederick slapped his wing tips to his forehead and shook his head in exasperation. He returned to his closet, shuffled a few items on hangers, and grabbed some clothing. Garments flew through the air. Soon a pile of clothes were scattered all around the ground.

At last, Frederick pulled out two bulky, colorful outfits. "I knew these would come in handy one day! And that day is... ta-da...today!"

Frederick held up what looked like two unicorn costumes. The large fur covered costumes had a tuft of rainbow hair that came down in swooping waves. When the light caught the rainbow hair just right, it glittered in the sun.

Soma and the egrets looked at each other in disbelief. They were simply speechless.

Thunder tilted his head at him in confusion. "What's that?"

"It's a unicorn suit, silly!"

Thunder scratched his head with his trunk wondering if Frederick expected them to put those on. "Are you sure? I don't like the sound of this."

Soma gave Frederick an ice laden glare. "Unicorns don't exist."

"Of course. I know that! Don't you get it? If they don't exist, then no one can see you! Voila!" gestured Frederick with his hand.

Cedric blinked. "Is that how it really works?"

"Oh, right! And I suppose you want her to wear the pretty pink and purple one."

Frederick nodded affirmatively, "That's right, of course! They'll never know!"

Soma shook her head. "That's ridiculous!"

Cedric bounded up to Soma's head and knocked on it. "Listen, sister. You've got to do this to get us through!"

Soma snorted at him. "Tell me something new."

Frederick threw a unicorn outfit over Thunder. He smoothed the fur out and whistled to himself. Then he tossed the other outfit over Soma. He ignored her stamping feet. "I feel just like a stage mother! Oh, how exciting! Oh!"

Meanwhile, the egrets were sneaking under Soma's costume in an attempt to get covered up. After a few seconds, they were too hot under all the fur and struggled to get out from under the costume on Soma's back. They ended up in a pile on the ground under Soma.

Frederick found a giant cone-shaped object and fitted it over Soma's horn. "There. Now you are ready! Ready for the ball, my princess! And don't you forget to take it to the dry cleaners before returning it to moi."

Soma rolled her eyes at him and muttered, "Why did I even get up this morning? Cleaners...I'll take something to the cleaners, all right."

Thunder's words came out muffled and nasally from beneath the costume. "Can we go now?"

Penelope whistled above them. "Time to fly. Time to fly. Let's go."

CHAPTER 19
SLINGSHOT

The egrets were now walking around Soma and laughing as they pointed at her goofy costume. Soma's cheeks turned red and she started to chase them. Sensing that they better find cover, they fluttered away.

When Sydney landed back on Soma, she accidentally stepped on a loose thread from Soma's costume. She was laughing so hard at the costume that her eyes were squeezed shut, and she did not even know that her feet were unraveling the unicorn outfit.

Soma whipped around to face her head-on, her eyes crossed and steam was coming out of her nose and ears. Sydney opened her eyes and saw Soma in front of her. When she noticed the unraveled costume she gulped. "Oops."

Sydney lifted her foot off the thread. Like a boomerang, it shot out from under her. The thread stretched out and yanked Soma in the other direction. Sydney fell off and tumbled on the ground.

Frederick shook his head pathetically. "Oh, brother. We've got a live one here."

Cedric shook his head at her. "Soma, you've got to take

this seriously. Stop playin' around."

Soma shot him a dirty look.

Frederick rolled his eyes at the spectacle, then clapped his wings to get their attention. "Alright, alright, class, on to the next idea. Time to take it to the next level! Get out of the shallow end, if you know what I mean. And that means you, with the pointy protrusion. You know, you could hang things on that husky hook of yours!"

Frederick stood next to Soma. "Now, let's see. What to do, what to do? Back to the drawing board. Hm. Large, round body, spear in head. What else can we do? Oy! Not much!"

Rolling his eyes, Frederick stepped away from her. He sashayed over to a sandy area surrounding the lagoon and used a toe claw to draw blueprints in the sand. Frederick drew what looked like complicated mathematical equations. He muttered to himself, "Hm. Let's see. How about a hut? A boat? A tow truck? Dump truck?"

Soma scowled back at Frederick's suggestions. "That one's gone around the bend."

"No...wait!! I've got it! Spandex!!" Frederick held his wing tip up as if he had the world's best idea.

"Wait, what?" Soma's head snapped around to look at the flamingo. "And what about my horn?"

Frederick shrugged his shoulders. "Small detail. No worries!"

"Is this new idea gonna get me home?" Thunder asked him.

"Honey, home is where you want it to be." Frederick returned to his closet. He opened a large trunk and peeled through more layers of clothes.

"Aha! I knew they were in here somewhere!" Frederick pulled out a pair of black yoga pants and held them up. "This is your ticket out! Come with me!"

Soma groaned and shook her head. "Oh, no, no, no."

"Oh, yes, yes, yes, yes, yes!" returned Frederick.

Soma looked cross-eyed at Frederick. "You're kidding, right?"

The egrets, all now sitting on her back again, broke out in laughter.

Persius hooted the loudest. "We should have tickets for this show!"

Frederick snapped his fingers. "Come stand over here! I don't have all day." Frederick pointed to a spot between two trees. He stretched the yoga pants between the trees. He planned to use the yoga pants as a slingshot to propel Thunder and Soma across the field.

Thunder and Soma walked over to the trees then stood on their hind legs, side by side before the pants. They leaned back into the spandex yoga pants and waited to see what would happen next.

Frederick pulled the yoga pants until they were taut. Closing one eye, he squinted with the other, aiming the slingshot device at the far edge of the field away from the lagoon. "Just a little more to the left. Okay! And you thought you couldn't fly! Ah, ha, ha, ha, ha!"

Frederick released the yoga pants sling. *Thwang!* Thunder and Soma jettisoned through the air. Thunder's ears flapped loudly in the wind as their two big bodies soared over the field.

Penelope, the egrets, and Frederick watched them catapult through the air.

"Are they gonna make it?" Cedric asked.

The answer came soon enough. Thunder and Soma landed just short of the edge of the field, in a muddy area. *SPLAT!!*

Persius shook his head. "Destination not reached."

Soma rolled over and glared back over in their direction. As soon as she could, she stood up and charged toward the forest.

Cedric nodded to the others. "Okay, time to fly! Let's go!"

"See ya, Frederick!" said Persius.

Penelope blinked her eyes. "Bye, bye big birdy."

Frederick waved at them. "Don't forget me when you write your memoirs!"

Penelope and the egrets took off over the field. Soma was charging so fast, they could not catch up to her.

"Hey, Ms. Soma! Hello!?" Cedric called from above.

"Whoa, sister! Wait for us!" Persius added.

Sydney had trouble getting her words out. "I can't… hiccup…I can't keep up!"

Persius flew up behind Sydney where she could not see him. "Boo!!"

Now startled, Sydney fell a few feet. "What are you doin'?"

"Tryin' to scare the hiccups." Persius heard her hiccup again as she flew in the air above Soma. "So much for that idea."

"Wait for me!" Thunder called from far back.

"We're on our own. She's not stopping for *anyone!*"

All of the birds circled above. Thunder got up and trotted across the field. He was very excited. Today, he just might find his mother again. "I can't wait for you to meet my mom! She's the best! I think we're almost there!"

Back at Frederick's pad, the flamingo was putting on his

makeup at the vanity in his outdoor dressing room. "Let's see how my pupils are doing. Yes! Yes!"

Frederick strolled away from his lagoon and flew over to the border fence. He gingerly lifted his wing to shade his eyes. Scanning the field, he caught Penelope, the egrets, Thunder, and Soma in his sights as they made their way from open land and back into the covered forest.

He hooted in glee. "Woohooo-ooo. It worked! It worked!! I should patent those yoga pants." Strolling back to his digs, he plucked a flower and smelled it. "This is the perfume for moi! Aahh."

CHAPTER 20
WHERE'S PENELOPE?

Racing after Soma, Thunder was now completely out of breath. He panted through his mouth as he stopped short. Penelope and the three egrets landed on Thunder. Soma had finally slowed down her pace, but she was still moving ahead of them.

Thunder picked a branch of ripe, red berries with his trunk. Hurrying to catch up with her, he planted himself in front of her. He raised the branch in the air. "Here. These are for you for trying to help me." He knew she must still be angry about flying through the air like that.

Soma quickly inhaled the entire branch until there was nothing left. "Mmmm."

Cedric shook his head at her. "You could at least say thank you."

"Yeah, Ms. Soma," agreed Persius.

Soma burped. "Mmm, mm, mm." Another loud burp followed. "Thanks. The berries were delish."

Penelope looked at the berries on the bush off to the side. She leapt off Thunder's back, fluttered over to a bush nearby, and lunged forward to grab one. In doing so, she fell into a hunter's bird trap.

"Parrot down. Parrot down." Penelope tried to tip over the box with her beak. The box bounced around in the air, but she could not get out. Peeking through a small hole, she saw Thunder, Soma, and the egrets walking away. They were too far away to hear her now.

Thunder turned around and noticed that Penelope had disappeared from sight. "Penelope?"

The egrets who were now perched on top of Soma turned around. Cedric was the first to speak. "Hey, what happened?"

Persius shrugged his shoulders. "Where'd she go?"

Thunder darted here and there, looking up, down, and all around the trees. He too, disappeared from sight, but the others could still hear him. "Penelope! Penelope!!"

Soma started to help with the search. "Penelope?"

Sydney scratched her head with her wing tip. "Looks like she flew the coop!"

"I don't know. Something happened." Soma was always the naysayer of the group.

Thunder started to panic. "Penelope!!"

"Look, kid, she's gone. Kaput," Cedric said.

Sydney and Persius both jumped off Soma and hovered above them. In the distance, Persius saw what looked like the upright that Thunder had described earlier. Persius stopped mid-flight. "Uprights! Look! Over there!"

Sydney jumped back while up in the air, and she almost lost her flight in the process. "Aagghh! Let's get outta here!!"

Soma shrugged her shoulders. "I've got my horn."

"What about Penelope?" Thunder asked them.

"She's nowhere to be found, Thunder," Sydney answered.

"No matter now. We have to move on." Soma warned them.

"She's right. We can't wait for her! Run!! Fly!!" Persius called.

Thunder shook his head sadly. "I hope she comes back. I want her to meet my mom."

Thunder and Soma raced through the forest. The egrets grabbed a hold of Soma's ears as they were being jostled hard on her back.

"Stopppppppp! I can barely hold on!" Cedric complained.

Thunder and Soma come to a halt. They had put quite a distance between themselves and the upright poacher in their mad dash through the forest.

"I think we're safe now. Whew!" Sydney wiped sweat from her brow with her wing. All three of the egrets were shaken up. Their heads rotated as the dizziness cleared from them. When they tried to stand up, their legs were wobbly and they all fell over on top of each other. *Kerplunk!*

They decided to stay there for a moment to catch their breath. If they were lucky, maybe Penelope would fly back to them.

Meanwhile, in the small village, the occupants were gathered under a large open tent in the community meeting area. They were devastated that the fences had not kept the elephants out. Even though many had tried to get them to destroy the elephants in the past, there were still quite a few people determined that they could find another way to solve the problem without destroying the beautiful creatures.

Storm clouds rolled in overhead, blocking the sunlight from the sky. A bleak sign to those who were already feeling powerless. They had far too much rain lately.

One man stood at the front of the group, trying to get them to calm down, but the people were too upset to let him speak.

"We need more fences!" He called out to them.

"Yeah!" replied another.

"More barricades!!" shouted another voice.

"We must stop them at all costs!" This voice wanted more than walls to keep the creatures out. He wanted them dead.

"I agree! We must change the law!"

Loud chaos erupted as a light wind blew. The people continued to argue about their course of action. Chimes tingled absently.

The voices did not stop until a large gust of wind nearly blew the tent over. Lightning cracked across the sky and thunder erupted in a loud *BOOM* in the distance. All the heads turned to look up at the sky. Their arguments no longer mattered. The storm approaching was more urgent.

The storm clouds hovered and a brief silence followed before a sudden downpour breached the line of the clouds. The weather had turned ugly real fast. The villagers raced to their homes, dodging the large pelting drops along the way.

Imani was outside the shack playing with her puppy, Senji, when the storm first struck. Her dog was chasing an African Striped Squirrel across their plot of land.

"Senji! Senji! Come back!"

Imani started to follow Senji into the forest when the storm first broke out. She continued to chase him all way down to a nearby river bank. The rain poured harder than Imani had ever seen. Before long, the river was swelling before her.

As the storm surge continued, Imani called to Senji. "Here,

Senji! Come!"

The dog was shivering on the spit in the middle of the river. Imani knew that if she did not act quickly, her dog would be swept up and away. Imani crossed to where he was and swept him up in her arms. When she turned around, she saw a large gush of water bursting closer to them.

The water level rose so high, that Imani and Senji were trapped on the spit. She knew that she could not across. "Help! Help! Papa! Help!!"

Imani looked out towards her family's field. She snuggled into Senji's fur and held him tight against her. They were both soaked to the bone. She was frightened, and all she wanted to do was go home, but it all looked so hopeless. Sitting down on the spit, she started to cry softly. How was she ever going to get home?

CHAPTER 21
THE WATERING HOLE

Their small group rested in the rainforest. The egrets were sitting on Soma, who was chomping down on more leaves. A flash of light filtered down through the rainforest, followed by a loud rumble. While the sounds of an impending storm erupted around them, none of the rain had actually touched the forest floor.

Thunder was plopped down next to Soma worrying about Penelope when he saw Jennetta Blue fly by him. He smiled at the butterfly who had been his silent companion for all his young life. He stood up quickly and followed after her. "Hey! Come back!"

Jennetta Blue fluttered up into the trees almost completely from sight. Thunder stopped in his tracks. Large leaves shaped like his own ears brushed against his trunk. "I remember these!"

He turned to the others. "Hey! Over here! Look! I think we're close!"

Without warning, the upright, Drago, crashed through the bushes with his rifle in one hand and rope in another. "Now I've got you. You're gonna make me rich!"

Thunder froze in his tracks. He shivered in fear. When would they finally be free from the uprights that chased after them? What had they ever done to these uprights?

Soma chafed her hooves. She did not have any questions in her head. Not a single one. Instead, she huffed from her nostrils and prepared to charge at Drago. The egrets jumped up and flew away from Soma's rear.

"Hey, you! Stop or we'll peck you to death!" Cedric shouted at him.

"Ack!!" Yelled Sydney.

Persius snarled at Drago. "Argh!!"

Drago aimed his rifle up at Cedric. His finger was on the trigger when Sydney and Persius swooped down and pecked at his head. Sydney grabbed a hunk of hair between her beak and started ripping strands away from his head.

Drago turned and swiped at them. "Aarrgghh!! Get away!!"

Soma took that moment to charge him. She made a mad dash at him, but Drago stepped aside at the last second. Soma missed him and rammed right into a tree with her horn stuck inside it.

Thunder watched in horror. "Soma!"

Cedric called out to him, "Help us, Thunder!"

Thunder trembled slightly. "What should I do?"

"Help Soma get free!" Cedric ordered.

Sydney and Persius continued to barrage Drago with bombing attacks. They dived down and pecked at any part of them they could reach. Drago waved his arms wildly, trying to protect his head from the attacking birds. He took one more swing at them, but they attacked him from all sides.

Drago's gun went off. Crack! Flocks of birds in the trees were flushed out from the forest. Their cries filled the forest in loud chirps, shrieks, and squawks. Before long the noises stopped as all the birds scattered from sight.

Drago dropped his rifle when Sydney pecked at his wrist. He tried to grasp her around the neck. "I'll get you! Aarrgh!"

Thunder ran to the tree where Soma was stuck. He pulled one of the branches with his trunk. He bent it over until it snapped. "I'm trying, Soma. I'm trying!"

Soma pulled back as hard as she could. She yanked and tugged with all her might until she finally freed herself. A heavy branch broke off from above and came crashing down, barely missing them.

Soma turned around and charged directly at Drago. Her jagged horn pierced him in the rear.

Drago fell forward, completely caught off guard. He quickly pushed up to his feet and took off running. The egrets that were swarming him before continued to harass him. "Aauurrgghh!!"

"We've got him on the run! Go, Thunder, go!" cheered Cedric.

"You, too, Ms. Soma!" shouted Persius.

"Yeah! We're right behind you!!" Sydney soared after them.

Thunder and Soma hurried off. The egrets continued to chase Drago away. He disappeared into the foliage. When they were done, the egrets returned to Soma and landed on her backside.

Light rain started to fall through the forest canopy. The trickling water was a reprieve from the fear that raced through them. It was like a healing balm, even to the egrets who hated getting wet.

"Whew!" said Cedric.

"Whoa! What a workout!" added Persius.

145

"Yeah, but it was kinda fun, wasn't it?" asked Sydney.

Persius grabbed a giant palm frond with his beak, tearing it off as they passed. He used it as an umbrella. All three egrets huddled under it while crouching on Soma's back.

Persius glared at Sydney. "Fun? Are you nuts?"

Sydney chuckled. "Just as nuts as you for even being here!"

Thunder peered behind him to see if Drago was following them. "Do you think he'll come back?"

"He'd be a fool to now. Look at the sky," answered Persius.

They peered up and saw more lightning flashes. They heard thunder cracking followed by a steady flow of rain. Puddles formed quickly around them.

"Which way to the herd?" Cedric asked Thunder.

Thunder turned his head and looked around him. "That way…I think." Thunder pointed his trunk ahead of him then stopped. Turning around, another worry filled his head. "But what about Penelope?"

Soma gave him a pitying glance. "Keep moving. No time to waste, Thunder."

Thunder sighed. He sure hoped that Penelope was all right. He already missed her cheerful banter.

As the group traveled deeper into the forest, the air around them was darker as the sun that had once filled the sky no longer filtered down through the trees. The buzz of life was quiet too, since the animals were now occupied with keeping themselves dry under their hidden shelters.

Thunder looked ahead and saw the familiar break in the tree line. "I see it! It's over there!"

Thunder trotted off ahead of Soma and the egrets. He came up to the forest edge and out to his herd's watering hole. When he looked around him, he was confused. "Huh?"

Soma and the egrets caught up to him and stopped in their tracks. They were now standing at the edge of a clearing.

They sat in there soaking in the rain as they took in the sight in front of them. None of them could dare speak of the decimation they saw in front of them. Trees had toppled, their exposed core displayed jagged edges. The bushes had been trampled and the flowers that had once been full of life now lay wilted on the ground. The pond that had been filled with enough water to be drench you on a hot day was now nearly dried up. There was no sign of life, only large scattered footprints followed by much smaller ones.

Sydney's eyes were huge. "What happened here?"

Cedric shook his head in disbelief. "Yeah, not much left."

"No birds?" asked Sydney.

"They've flown the coop, sister." Persius replied.

Tears were welling up in Thunder's eyes. "My herd! They can't be gone!! They must be here somewhere!"

Thunder dashed from one side of the clearing to the other. He searched everywhere around him for any sign of his herd. They had to be alive still, they just had to. He rushed between the forest and clearing, back and forth he zigged and zagged. He found scrape marks that indicated something large had been dragged.

He remembered the chaos of when the uprights had come into his life. The loud trumpeting elephants that tried to escape their attackers, the ones who had fallen to the earth, and the loud explosions that had filled the air. He remembered some of the elephants being pulled across the ground. "Huh!! Oh no!"

Thunder collapsed on the ground and all the joy he had left in his body evaporated. He was now filled with the desolation that one could only feel with the breaking of his heart. Big, fat tears rolled down his face, staining the wrinkled skin with his sadness. The raindrops fell hard on his head, but Thunder could no longer feel them. He was numb to their touch. Loud sobs came from his chest and burst from his trunk as he trumpeted a sad, lonely call. "Mother!"

A tear left the corner of Soma's eye. The hardened rhino could not stand to see Thunder this way. "Those uprights!"

Cedric was uncomfortable with the emotional display before him. He tried to push it away. "Now what do we do?"

Thunder turned to look at him. "They're gone! Our watering hole! My herd! My mom! Gone." Thunder moved slowly along the edge of the pond, with his head down and his trunk almost touching the ground. His heavy heart was matched by his large feet that left prints in the sand. He sunk down next to the water and his trunk splashed into it.

Soma plodded over to Thunder and stood over him. His quiet snuffling tore at her hardened heart. She breathed a comforting snort of air on his ear and Thunder shrugged it off.

The egrets came out from under the palm frond and jumped down to perch at Thunder's feet. One of his tears plopped down on Sydney's toe and she did not even bother to shake it free.

Thunder did not want to feel so helpless. "We have to keep looking. Where's Penelope? And why did she leave us? We're lost without her! Penelope!!!!! Where are you?" He called for his friend as loud as he could.

Up above them a loud shrill answered. Penelope had broken free from her trap moments before and had been searching for her friends. She did not notice the devastation down on the ground. She was simply happy to see Thunder.

Penelope saw the egrets on Thunder's outstretched feet and dived down to meet them. When she landed, Penelope jumped up and down, happy to see them. Her voice was enthusiastic, "Penelope's back. How's it goin'? Guess what? Guess what? Guess what? Guess what?"

Penelope stepped up onto Thunder's outstretched trunk and reached for his ears. She pulled them so that he brought his face closer. Thunder's grief shaken mind cleared for a moment for the parrot had completely caught him off guard.

Penelope saw the trail of tears running down his face. She reached her wing out to touch them and raised her wing tip to inspect it more closely. She looked up at his face again then back down to the tear stained feathers.

Hopping down from his trunk, she turned to face him. "Where's the party?"

Penelope hopped over to the water's edge and looked at both their faces in the water. She tapped the water with her foot and small rings rippled around it.

Thunder looked up dejectedly. "They're all gone—all of them."

Penelope tilted her head at him. "No one's home. No dinner. Not tonight." Penelope stepped closer to Thunder and snuggled against his foot. It was the closest thing she could give him to a hug.

Soma sniffed and tried to hide the tear in the corner of her eye. She reigned in her emotions and reached deep down to find the anger that normally fueled her. "Not anymore. Only death and destruction. The uprights again."

"Not good," replied Cedric.

Sydney shook her head. "This changes everything."

Cedric shook his head. "That's right."

A dog barked in the distance. They turned to look at the interruption. The dog howled through the rain then started to bark loudly again. A female child was crying out for her uprights to save her. "Help!! Help!!"

"Huh? What's that?" Thunder recoiled. The egrets now startled, leapt from Thunder's feet as he jumped up and raced through the forest.

"Aahh! Run for cover!!" called Sydney. The egrets scuttled over to Soma and landed on her backside.

"Let's go, Ms. Soma," said Persius.

"Yeah. Let's get outta here," suggested Cedric.

Soma grumbled and started to move as the sound of the young girl's voice carried through the forest. Penelope soared through the air and hopped back onto Thunder's head.

"What is that?" asked Cedric.

"Someone's in trouble," Persius replied.

Soma huffed loudly. "Leave 'em be. We need to stay hidden. Danger is everywhere."

Thunder ignored Soma and continued to move forward. Soma had no choice but to follow.

Chapter 22
Thunder to the Rescue

Thunder continued to move down the path. It led them out to a river where they saw Imani frozen with fear. With nowhere to go, the water continued to gather around her. The African Striped Squirrel the dog had chased down to the water know hurled himself onto a log and floated down the river escaping the treacherous flood.

Thunder pointed to the girl with his trunk. "Look! That little upright is in danger!"

Soma shrugged her shoulders. She saw no need to help the child. "Others will come and save it. If they see us, they'll take us, too!"

Persius shook his head at Soma. "Man, you're a hard one!"

Sydney tapped her foot on Soma's back. "I know your problem. Not enough maternal love. Father gone. Wrong kind of attention. You know the story…"

Soma was now perturbed. "Rhinos are rugged by nature!"

Cedric moved to stand onto Soma's horn. He faced her head-on and pointed a wing tip at her. "Don't you think you could soften that tough hide and prehistoric attitude long enough to show you have a heart?!"

Soma scowled and puffed up. "Hmph! Pft!"

Soma's strong breath blew Cedric right off her horn. He toppled backwards in the air and tumbled to the ground. "You're sooo prickly! Geez!"

"Let it go. She's not changing anytime soon." Sydney shook her head.

Thunder continued to stare at the small upright. After all they had been through, Soma's words rang true, but he couldn't walk away. "I can't leave her there."

The group watched in shock as Thunder disregarded Soma's advice and tried to cross the swiftly flowing water.

Mosi rode his bicycle home from the village, but with the torrential downpour he was drenched by the time he got there. After entering his shack, he returned outside moments later. Where was Imani? Where was his little girl?

Mosi cupped his hands and yelled, "Imani!"

Mosi ran around the surrounding area. Panic rose in his chest. "Imani!!"

He dashed out across the field toward the river pelted by hard rain every step of the way.

When he caught a glimpse of three male adult elephants at the water's edge he forgot Imani for a moment. He raced back into the house and came out with Drago's rifle. He headed toward the river intent on solving his elephant problem once and for all.

Thunder charged ahead through the swiftly moving

current. Swimming up onto the spit, he approached Imani and Senji. He ran around them in a circle trying to figure out what to do. How could he make contact with her?

Imani watched him in awe. Reaching out her hand, she waited to see what Thunder would do.

Thunder raised his trunk to her hand and sniffed it. When she did not move, Thunder took that as a good sign. Surely, this tiny upright would not hurt him. He recognized the fear in her eyes. He had carried the same fear with him the minute he had been snatched away from his herd. This one here, she was an innocent like him. Thunder lifted his trunk to her head and patted it gently.

Imani smiled through her tears as if to say hello. It was a hidden language, one that had been lost over the years. Man to beast, heart to heart, a reminder that they may have different shapes and sizes, but they all had beating hearts. They loved, they feared, they lost in pretty much the same ways.

At this point, the adult elephants were wading into the river and out toward the spit. They saw Thunder and looked at each other curiously. They had never seen an upright so casual with their kind. The only experience they had with man was the kind that made them want to run away. The sight of Thunder and the child sharing a mutual respect for each other made them wade closer to him.

Mosi continued to follow after the elephants. He recognized Imani and Senji on the spit with an elephant calf near her, and he felt panic seize him. The elephants he had been following were now moving slowly through the raging water toward Imani. He feared they would see Imani as a threat to the calf. Imani and Senji were trapped there on the spit with the wild animals that had destroyed their farm. He had to protect her.

In a panic, Mosi looked around for a way to get out to the spit. Water gathered around him, covering his feet. He was soon up to his knees in it. There was no way he could move quickly or easily through it. He fell down trying to walk through the raging water.

Mosi stood up again. He dove into the water and tried to swim over to his daughter. It was a futile attempt for the water pushed him downstream and his body contorted painfully against its wicked flow. When Mosi thought the raging water would claim him, he managed to reach for a branch above him. Using pure will, he pulled himself up from the rapids bursting around him. Climbing away from the river, he landed safely on the shore.

Near the river, the egrets waddled up from Soma's back and perched themselves on her forehead to get a closer look at Thunder across the stream.

"What's he doing?" asked Sydney.

"Uh-oh. He's gone over!" called Cedric.

"Thunder!! Come back!"

Soma grunted. "I don't think we should get involved."

Persius pointed with his wing, "Look!!"

Penelope squawked overhead. "On a mission. Go! Go! Go!"

The elephants were now near the spit. They greeted Thunder with low, soft rumbles. One of them sniffed and patted him on the back with his trunk. They nudged Thunder closer.

One elephant grabbed Thunder's tail with his trunk and Thunder knew he was meant to follow them. Thunder knelt down so Imani could climb up on him. The child gave him a cautious glance before she climbed on his back. Senji barked and leapt into Imani's arms.

Thunder felt the child hanging on tight to the folds of skin around his neck. The male elephants surrounded Thunder as he entered the water with Imani and her dog on his back. All of them proceeded slowly across the river. Thunder knelt down again under a tree so Imani and Senji could dismount in a safe place.

The water raged so violently that the spit they were just on was now submerged. Imani was watching with wide eyes. She ran a hand along Thunder's ear and smiled up at him. "Thank you, my friend."

Mosi had seen Thunder and the elephants carry Imani and Senji to safety. He also saw the trust his daughter had with the creatures. None of the elephants were going to hurt her. They were not the creatures that Drago had created in his head. They were simply trying to survive the same way he was. His anger and fear was replaced with something else: disgust. He had always promised to preserve and protect the things that could not protect themselves. He let the rifle fall from his grasp into the raging water where the current swiftly took it downstream. The majestic elephants before him deserved much more than he could ever provide, but he had time to make a difference and he would if it was the last thing he did.

CHAPTER 23
TALL TREASURES

Imani and Mosi watched the elephants from a distance, and Imani squeezed his arm tight when Thunder fell into the water. When the large elephants went in to save him, they sat in awe of the moment.

"Look, Papa! Tall treasures!! I want to go and talk to them!

Mosi chuckled at her. He ran his hand over her cheek. "Well, Imani. We have to give them their space."

Imani looked up at him with her innocent face. "Papa, you're not going to shoot them, are you?"

Mosi flushed with guilt. He had not even realized his daughter had known his original plan. Shame filled him. "No, baby, no. There will be no more shooting. Not if I can help it."

And for the first time in a long time, Mosi knew he would have to change his ways. It was time to learn how to live in peace with the animals around him. Balance would have to return.

Later, as the flood waters started to recede, Mosi, Imani

and Senji trailed back to their shack. Imani and Senji ran inside. Mosi grabbed his bicycle and turned it upside down. He picked up a tool to work on its bent wheel. At that moment, Drago's truck pulled up next to him

Drago gestured to him from the window. "Are you ready for another job?"

Mosi shook his head at him and stood up in a firm stance. "No, Drago. I'll not be shooting anything. Your gun is gone!"

Drago sneered at Mosi. "I want my rifle replaced!"

Mosi dropped his tools and crossed his arms in front of him. "No, cousin. No more killing! We have to take care of them! Don't you understand?!"

Drago shook his head in disgust. "You're a fool, Mosi. You will continue to suffer."

"I would rather suffer than destroy another living being. I will find another way. And the others will listen to me when I tell them my story."

A huff of air left Drago's mouth before he grinned. "Yeah, right. Money talks, cousin."

"How many shiny, new things do you need to be happy?"

Drago stared down at him without responding. Momentary silence passed between them. He rolled up his window and drove off, the frustration etched clear across his face.

CHAPTER 24
GOOD-BYE DEAR FRIEND

Penelope hopped around Thunder. "Everyone okay? Time for a shower?"

"Yes, Penelope. I'm all right..." Thunder looked around. "But where's Soma?"

The egrets were perched together on a rock nearby. Their eyes scanned the wreckage created by the raging waters.

"She was right here. Where'd she go?" asked Cedric.

Sydney shook her head. "I thought you were with her."

"Uh-oh. I thought *you* were with her." Persius added.

Cedric was starting to worry. "Where'd she go? She was right here a minute ago!"

The birds flew up and scanned the area from above. Thunder stood up and looked around too. He sniffed the air, hoping to pick up her scent.

"Ms. Soma! Ms. Soma!" called Sydney.

"Probably saw some irresistible berries. Couldn't help herself. You know Ms Soma." Cedric added.

"Or she went off to find a new mud puddle!" Persius agreed.

Sydney nodded her head. "Yeah, that's probably it."

161

"Let's head for the trees. Better views!" Cedric suggested.

The egrets fluttered up to a tall fig tree. Penelope headed back along the river's edge. She noticed a gigantic fallen tree with a large animal under its massive branches.

"Uh-oh, uh-oh, uh-oh." Penelope whistled.

Thunder ran along below Penelope. The egrets jumped down from the tree and onto Thunder's back for a ride. Thunder looked ahead of them. "Could that be...? Huh? Oh no!"

Penelope landed on the downed tree and saw Soma. "How ya doin,' Soma? How ya doin,'Soma? Wake up."

Thunder and the egrets arrived next to her. The egrets leapt from Thunder's back, one at a time and walked in a line and onto the fallen tree.

Sydney approached Soma's partially covered body. Her face was downcast as she realized that Soma was not moving. She tried to pry one of the branches free. The other egrets leapt over the branch on top of her and wrangled their way under it.

Cedric pecked at Soma's ear, but there was no response. "Ms. Soma?"

Sydney landed on her horn and tried to open her eyelids with her beak. Soma's eyes were fixated in a blank stare. "Huh?!!"

Sydney stepped back, fear tingling her feather tips. She marched back and forth along the branch.

When Persius flew up onto Soma's torso, he jumped up and down on her side, trying to get Soma to breath. He repeated his actions over and over.

"C'mon, old girl," cried Sydney.

They sat there, hoping for some kind of miracle that never came. Soma did not react to them whatsoever.

Cedric plopped down on the ground and shook his head sadly. "She's...she's gone."

Sydney gasped. "You mean she's..."

Persius wrapped a wing around Sydney. "I'm afraid so, sister."

Thunder joined them. He did not understand why they were so sad. "Is she asleep?"

Realizing that Thunder had not much experience with death, Cedric cleared his throat. "Well...she's not coming back, little Thunder. That's all I can say."

The egrets cried on each other's wings. Thunder used his trunk to gather the birds closer to him. He wept with them as their words finally caught on.

Penelope cocked her head left to right, confused by the display. "Ding! Dong! Wake up, Soma."

Jennetta Blue flew overhead and hovered around Soma's lifeless body. Thunder noticed the butterfly through his ears. His eyes widened in awe. He spoke directly to his tiny friend. "It's going to be okay, right?"

Jennetta Blue hovered momentarily and flapped her wings. She flew all around Soma's body, as if preparing her soul to travel up to the sky. After a moment, Thunder almost thought he saw a small mist rise around the rhino. It rose up into the air and Jennetta Blue rose with it. Her tiny wings ushered Soma's spirit up and away as she flittered away.

"Good-bye Ms. Soma...I will miss you."

CHAPTER 25
AN ESCORT HOME

Back up the river, the male elephants still remained. They were quietly standing by in the distance on the other side of the river.

Cedric looked away from Soma and gestured. "Look! The big elephants are still here!"

"What are they doin'?" Persius wondered.

"You mean, what are they waitin' for?" asked Sydney.

"Me," Thunder said softly as he peered down at Soma. He gazed out at the elephants and rumbled his feet on the ground.

The elephants responded in soft, low tones. They approached Thunder and the birds, and bowed low before Soma with their trunks still lifted in the air to pay respects to the soul that had passed into the afterlife.

The elder elephant spoke softly to Thunder. "Come with us, now. We'll show you the way."

Thunder looked back and forth between the elephants and his friends. He did not want to leave them, but he needed to find his herd. He needed his mother now more than ever. Thunder trumpeted lightly. The other two male elephants trumpeted back. Thunder turned to his friends with tears in his eyes. "I have to go with them."

Penelope tilted her head at him. "Home's not here? Where's home?"

Thunder pointed with his trunk. "I think it's over there… somewhere."

"Coming back?" Penelope cooed at him. "See you again?"

Thunder shrugs sadly.

"See him again? I'm going *with* him!!" Sydney answered. She was still sad by the loss of her friend, but life had to go on. Soma would want it that way.

Cedric agreed. He too would miss the grumpy rhino, but there was nothing they could do about her loss now. "Aha! Great idea! Lots of tasty morsels to pick off those massive bags of skin! I'm in!"

Persius was having a harder time departing. "But what about Ms. Soma? We can't just leave her here!"

"We have no choice, Persius. This is the cycle of life. We cannot take her with us now," answered Sydney.

"Let's cover her up with her favorite leaves and berry branches," suggested Cedric. It was a small tribute to such a fierce protector.

Sydney agreed. "Hey, little pachyderm. Help us, will ya?"

"Will she be okay here?" Thunder asked.

"Safe now," answered Penelope as she dropped a small flower on the top of the mound.

"Good-bye, Ms. Soma," Cedric sniffed as one last tear left his eye.

Sydney shifted on her feet uncomfortably as she tried to keep more tears from falling. Her voice choked up as she whispered, "G'bye, old girl."

Persius let his wing caress the mound before him. "Rest

in peace."

Cedric cleared his throat. "Okay. Let's go, Fellas!"

The egrets flew from the mound on top of Soma's body and landed on Thunder's back. Penelope stood alone on the ground next to Thunder's feet.

"Hey! Move over! I was here first!" Persius said to the other egrets.

Sydney gave him a forced grin. "All right, all right. Just keep your wings to yourself, will ya?"

"Relax you two. They'll be lots of room! Look! We'll each have our own first class seat assignments!" interrupted Cedric.

Sydney and Persius both broke out in laughter. They knew that everything would be all right.

"Yeah, that's right!"

Thunder nudged Penelope with his trunk. "Bye, Penelope. I won't ever forget you."

Penelope tapped his trunk with her beak a few times. "Coming back?"

Thunder gave her a goofy grin. "Of course! And we'll have another adventure!"

Penelope leapt up to Thunder's head. Looking him in the eye, she made kissing sounds. Thunder hugged Penelope with his ears.

The parrot jumped up from Thunder and flew to a large mahogany tree root base. She waved with her wing. "Find your mom? Find your mom?"

"Yes, I will," answered Thunder. He was even more determined to find her now. There was so much to tell her about. His friends. The surfing hippos. The uprights. The child and her dog.

The egrets waved back in unison and headed off with Thunder. Thunder trotted quickly over to the male elephants, which had already started to meander off.

The egrets fluttered off Thunder's back, unable to hold on. "Whoa, Nelly!" shouted Cedric. They each landed on a male elephant and found their own perches.

"Aahh! Much better!" said Persius.

Sydney gestured around her. "I got a room with a view!"

The male elephants rubbed up against Thunder as he neared them. They flapped their ears slowly against him.

Thunder giggled. "Hey, that tickles!"

The elder elephant spoke to Thunder. "Come with us. There's a herd ahead."

Thunder looks up at the elder elephant. "Is my mother with the herd?"

The elder elephant sighed softly. "I know not young one. Many of us didn't survive the attacks of the uprights on our herds." Thunder's ears fold back and a huge tear welled up in his eye. "Whatever you find when you get there, know this… we are your family now."

Thunder hung his head sadly.

"That was a brave thing you did back there saving the young upright. We are very proud of you. It took great strength and courage to do what you did, especially after what the uprights put you through. You've demonstrated wisdom well beyond our young years."

Thunder looked up and smiled at the praise. "Thank you, sir."

"No thanks necessary, young one. If even one upright has learned a lesson from all this, we will all reap the rewards."

"Why can't everyone just get along with each other?"

The elder elephant smiled at him. "If the uprights have learned a lesson from this there is still hope.

Thunder smiled again. "Hope…I like the sound of that."

The elder elephant chuckled softly. I do too. Now...let's pick up the pace. We still have a way to go."

CHAPTER 26
TUSKER'S PROPHECY FULFILLED

Moments later, they moved through the densely covered forest. A beautiful lake was just a few feet away.

Sydney pointed. "Look! A rainforest Riviera!"

Frederick, the flamingo, was sunning himself near the edge of the river. He was wearing a pair of sunglasses over his eyes, and had a cool, tropical drink in a wooden mug with a hollow reed for a straw. He sat on a chaise lounge made with woven reeds and had a magazine in his wing that looked like it had washed up from the beach.

"Look who's there!" gestured Persius.

"He knows all the best spots!" declared Cedric.

Sydney shook her head in agreement. "We should hang out with him more often!"

Frederick caught them from the corner of his eye and waved at the egrets from the chaise lounge. "Hello, boys!"

Sydney growled and placed her wings on her hips. Her foot was tapping impatiently as she glared at Frederick. "Do I look like a boy to you?"

"Uh, oh, Freddie, you've done it now," Cedrick said.

The other two egrets broke out laughing when Frederick

feigned being scared. Persius was laughing so hard, he doubled over and Sydney kicked him on the butt, knocking him off the elephant's back.

"Hey!" Persius shouted from the dusty ground.

Sydney looked around for any takers. "Who's next?"

Cedrick started backing up with his wings out in front to him to stay off Sydney's advances. He tripped over a fold in the elephant's skin and toppled over the side. "I shoulda seen that one comin'"

Frederick laughed at the egrets, and waived off Sydney's anger. "Girlfriend, you need to fly over to my pad later, and I'll show you a thing or two about how to dress the part. Pink...you know it's all the rave and all about the color. What do ya say?"

Sydney smiled. "You're on!"

Further in the forest, Penelope unlatched her nest door and entered. She tapped the firefly jar lid with her beak. The fireflies lit up and a low buzzing sound filled the air.

Penelope was in a melancholy mood. "Honey, I'm home."

She peeked in her mirror and pecked at it. "Woooo. Home is where the heart is. Wooo."

She looked around her empty nest. Everything was where she left it, but everything that had once been important to her no longer made her happy. She turned back to her reflection. "Home is where the heart is.... Heart is with Thunder. Woooo. Penelope go home."

Two silverback gorillas, Harold and Neville, had been observing from their hilltop vantage point. They saw the uprights building large fences around their farms. This time, they had taken down the electrical boxes that had been attached to them before.

Neville tilted his head as he watched them. "Uprights again? Hard to trust them."

Harold, "Yeah, you never know what they want."

Neville poked a twig into a termite mound. Small bugs gathered on the twig and he lifted it to his mouth. He slurped down the clinging tasty insects then dipped the stick back into the mound and handed the stick to Harold to share. Harold wiped his tongue across his lips.

"Mmm…" murmured Neville.

"Thanks!" Harold said.

Neville shook his head at the uprights below. "They need to wake up from their long sleep."

Harold nodded. "Seems they've forgotten their true purpose."

"And the original plan," agreed Neville.

"Maybe one day they will remember," added Harold.

"Perhaps," said Neville.

Harold and Neville heard the sound of hammering and noticed a female upright outside a scientist compound near the farms. She was putting the finishing touches on a large, open aviary.

"Look, some have. Ah, but some have not…"

The panoramic view of the rainforest was an amazing sight. Birds chirped happily around them. New night sounds started to break free as the sun started to set around them. Haru and the bats took flight across the sky. Elephants trumpeted in the distance.

"That's right," agreed Harold.

Thunder and his escorts entered the open valley. Out of nowhere Penelope flew in and landed on Thunder's head. "What the...?" Thunder said in surprise.

"Hi honey, I'm home. Woooo," Penelope chirped.

Both Thunder and the egrets laugh at the goofy parrot.

"Well, look what the cat dragged in," Sydney said.

"Welcome back, Penny," said Cedrick

When Penelope fisted her feathers at Cedrick's beak, they all laughed harder. "P-e-n-e-l-o-p-e."

"Okay, sorry, kid...er...Penelope," said Cedrick.

Penelope hopped onto Thunder's trunk and looked him in the eyes.

"Hi!" Thunder said.

Penelope cocked her head to the side. "Thunder find home?"

"Yes."

"Home is where the heart is. Woooo. Home is with Thunder." Thunder's smile grew as Penelope continued. "Thunder find mother?"

Thunder's smile faltered. "I will."

"Many elephant's ahead. Woooo. Thunder find mother."

Thunder looked past the bird into the field. Off in the distance he saw a large elephant herd, and his smile returned. "I see the herd, Penelope, my mom might be there!"

"Thunder find mother," Penelope chirped. "Thunder home."

Thunder stomped once, and the ground beneath their feet shook. Penelope flew up to land on Thunder's back. Thunder looked over to the elder elephant and he nodded in approval.

He stomped again and waited. One member of the herd stopped eating and looked up. At the third stomp the other elephant left the herd and headed in their direction at a run.

"Someone's coming!" Thunder stomped again in excitement Penelope flew off Thunder's back to join the egrets. "I think it's my mom...Yes, I see her!"

Thunder took off at a run toward her and met his mom in the middle of the field. Their trunks locked as they embraced. Sadness was replaced with joy. Their family had been reunited against all odds....

The rest of the herd acknowledged the happy reunion and encircled Serenity and Thunder. They raised their trunks and trumpeted gleefully in the air.

All the animals joined them in their celebration. Even Frederick paused to clap for their reunion. The egrets flew happy circles around them. The rest of the animals around the lake and near the edge of the forest were watching in awe.

Serenity was crying with happiness. "My baby, I thought I had lost you."

Thunder closed his eyes and nuzzled closer to her. "Home is where family is, and I'm never leaving you again."

"I love you, Thunder."

"Love you too, Mom, and boy did I have an adventure..."

The early morning sun was just cresting the horizon. A few dark storm clouds had gathered in the distance. Lightning flashed and thunder rolled over the countryside from the distance. A huge storm was brewing and would soon be upon them.

Thunder walked with Serenity and the elder elephant he now knew as Baron. They climbed up the gentle slope and stopped when they reached the top. They were high upon a bluff looking down over all the animals in the valley below. All the animals there were living in harmony.

Serenity rubbed her trunk affectionately over Thunder's head. He closed his eyes and leaned into her. "You've had quite an adventure, young man."

"I did, but all I really wanted to do was find you."

"Baron told me that you were brave out there and saved a young upright. I'm so proud of you."

"We all are," said Baron.

"You have grown into a fine young elephant, and it is an honor to call you my son."

Thunder smiled. "Thanks mom!"

BOOM! There was another flash of lightning and the thunder shook the ground. All the animals stopped what they were doing to look up into the sky. The clouds billowed and churned above them, then parted to show the great elephant, the legendary Tusker. Suddenly a great voice was heard. "Thunder, you have fulfilled the great legend bringing the animals and the uprights in harmony and peace for a moment in time. May we all learn from this and try to live in harmony from this day forward."

"Do you see that?" Baron asked. "That is the legendary Tusker.

Thunder's mouth had dropped open in awe. "Wow."

"You are now a legend. Your story will be told throughout our generations. Because of your selfless act of bravery, you have brought the hope of survival to the rainforest once again."

The end.

APPENDIX I

The threats to the elephant population, as of this writing, are very grave. Vulcan, a private company operating out of Seattle, Washington is dedicated to gathering accurate data on global issues, elephant predation being just one of them. Founded by Paul G. Allen, the group does in-depth very diverse research on climate change, sustainable communities, threats to our oceans, space travel, and Alzheimer's research, among others.

Their Great Elephant Census, the GEC, was recently completed (8/31/16) and the results were very disturbing. Their data indicated 352,271 African elephants now in 18 countries represented a 30% decline in that population within the last seven years.

Poaching, habitat loss, and the illegal ivory trade have created an alarming, continuous threat for this essential population. Action to remediate this blight needs to accelerate to reverse this destructive trend. In the Appendix II, we've listed some of the organizations dedicated to the conservation of elephants and other endangered species.

Drone surveillance to protect elephants and rhinos from poachers and to monitor herds is beginning to evolve in several African communities. This technology can provide actual evidence for criminal activity and create an immediate response protocol for law enforcement, along with its census taking and monitoring of the conditions for different animal groups. The "Air Shepard" concept is beginning to take hold in many places. Hopefully, more new technologies, along with greater public awareness, will evolve to support the protection of these unique animals.

APPENDIX: II

Groups that Support Elephant and Other Endangered Animal's Preservation within Sanctuaries, Rehabilitation Centers, and Medical Facilities.
This list was created by the group below:

DISAPPEARING ELEPHANTS
Exploring the threats to elephants around the world: An educational media portal created by the International Field Program of the New School

from their Website
The Amboseli Trust for Elephants aims to ensure the long-term conservation and welfare of Africa's elephants in the context of human needs and pressures through scientific research, training, community outreach, public awareness, and advocacy.

The African Conservation Foundation works to preserve Africa's wildlife by conducting, supporting, and linking conservation projects throughout the continent.

The African Wildlife Foundation is an international

conservation organization focusing their efforts across Africa. They work on promoting elephant conservation by reducing ivory consumption with their Say No Campaign, supporting anti-poaching efforts in Africa, and securing habitats across Africa's landscapes.

Big Life Foundation is a community based conservation organization that employs park rangers in Kenya and Tanzania to stop poaching in national parks. It works to protect all species in the parks, but elephants are the highest priority.

David Sheldrick Wildlife Trust and Elephant Orphanage is a sanctuary for orphaned elephants. The charity works closely with the Kenyan Wildlife Services to raise orphaned rhinos and elephants. Worry is their campaign started in Kenya that aims to protect elephants by raising awareness. They have campaign materials available for download.

Elephant Voices advances the study of elephant cognition, communication, and social behavior, promotes the scientifically sound and ethical management and care of elephants through research, conservation, education, and advocacy.

Elephants for Africa is a small charity dedicated to protecting African elephants through research and education projects in Botswana.

Save the Elephants is based in Kenya and works to secure a future for elephants and to sustain the beauty and ecological integrity of the places they live; to promote man's delight in their intelligence and the diversity of their world, and to develop a tolerant relationship between the two species. They

180

solely work to protect elephants.

Last Great Ape Organization is a non-governmental organization that works closely with governments to enforce and prosecute criminals who are involved in illegal wildlife trafficking.

SOS Elephants is dedicated to the preservation of elephants and their habitats throughout various regions by employing methods in research, education, conservation, and counter poaching disciplines. They are based in Chad and have an elephant orphanage.

Wildlife Direct is an international organization based in Kenya that works to protect African species and others around the world. It has organized two campaigns to protect elephants – Elephant Voices and Hands Off Our Elephants.

Bring the Elephant Home is an organization that works in Thailand to ensure the proper treatment of elephants in captivity and to promote the protection of wild elephants by securing their habitats.

Elephant Nature Park aims to provide a sanctuary and rescue center for Asian elephants. The sanctuary is in Chiang Mai, Northern Thailand.

ElefantAsia is an organization that aims to protect Asian elephants through different projects in Laos and Myanmar.

Save Elephant Foundation is dedicated to protecting Asian elephants. They are based in Thailand and work on local community outreach programs, rescue and rehabilitation programs, and educational ecotourism operations.

Sri Lanka Wildlife Conservation Society is an international community-based organization committed to the research, conservation and protection of Sri Lanka's endangered wildlife, communities, and natural habitats.

Surin Project is a new and innovative project focused on finding solutions to the challenges faced by mahouts and their elephants in Surin province in North-Eastern Thailand. It is committed to improving the living conditions of Asian elephants and providing sustainable economic revenue for their mahouts in the local community.

Wildlife Trust of India is a leading nature conservation organization committed to the service of nature. They partner with elephant-baring states, Asian Elephant Research and Conservation Centre (AERCC) and Project Elephant to provide corridors for elephant movement.

A Rocha India is an international conservation organization that works to protect the environment through local, community-based conservation, scientific research, and environmental education.

Burn the Ivory is a non-profit campaign that focuses on bringing awareness to elephant poaching crisis through educational outreach and advocacy and media campaigns. They raise funds to support conservation and anti-poaching efforts.

Elephant Aid International is a non-governmental organization that aims to raise global consciousness about the lives of elephants both in captivity and in the wild.

International Anti-Poaching Foundation is an Australian not-for-profit that has a military-like approach to conservation and anti-poaching. They work to prevent the wildlife trafficking of criminals.

The Kerulos Center is a non-governmental organization working to help animals The Billy and Kani Fund works to restore space, peace, and security for elephants and tribal communities.

The Nature Conservancy is an international organization that protects ecologically important lands and waters around the world. It also seeks to address threats to conservation involving climate change, fresh water, oceans, and conservation lands. It has specific efforts devoted to elephant conservation.

Think Elephants International is an organization focused on elephant conservation through education. They work to research cognitive behaviors of elephants and educate local and global youth about the threats to elephants.

WildAid works to raise awareness about wildlife trafficking in order to stop the demand for wildlife products. They campaign through video and other media and have support from many celebrities, including Yao Ming and Edward Norton.

The Wildlife Conservation Society (WCS) works to save

wildlife by addressing climate change; through natural resource exploitation; connecting wildlife health and human health; and supporting the sustainable development of human livelihoods. Their campaign focused on elephants, 96Elephants, seeks to garner support to protect the African elephant from poaching.

The US Fish & Wildlife Services have made efforts to burn US stockpiles of ivory and are funding international efforts to battle elephant poaching.

United States Environmental Protection Agency (EPA) is an independent campaigning organization committed to bringing about change that protects the natural world from environmental crime and abuse.

The World Wide Fund for Nature (WWF) is an international organization, with local offices in over 100 countries, dedicated to conserving nature. It seeks to reduce threats to biodiversity, protect and restore species and their habitats, help local communities conserve their natural resources, and reduce the impact of production and consumption on the natural world. It has specific efforts devoted to elephant conservation, with interesting and informative pages dedicated to African elephants and Asian elephants.
More WWF info: African elephants and Asian elephants

International Union for Conservation of Nature (IUCN) is a global conservation organization with over 200 government members and over 900 non-governmental members. It focuses on three areas: valuing and conserving nature, promoting effective and equitable governance of nature's use, and deploying nature-based solutions to global challenges in climate, food and development. It is not specifically focused on elephant conservation, but its researchers study many different species, including elephants. The IUCN is also referred to as World Conservation Union.

Conservation International (CI) is an international conservation organization that seeks to protect our natural wealth, promote sustainable production, and foster effective governance. Its goal is to protect what nature provides for humans: food, fresh water, livelihoods, and a stable climate. Its efforts are generally directed towards stopping illegal wildlife trade and are not focused only on elephants.

Convention on the International Trade in Endangered Species of Wild Fauna and Flora (CITES) is the international organization that implemented a complete trade ban of ivory, enacted in January 1990. CITES also established two monitoring groups to analyze how policies impact trade in elephant products. An overview of the two groups can be found here. The first group is MIKE – Monitoring the Illegal Killing of Elephants and the second is ETIS – the Elephant Trade Information System. CITES focuses on how wildlife trade affects populations of animals and, more specifically, elephant conservation.

International Fund for Animal Welfare (IFAW) is an international organization that works to protect animals around the world. It provides assistance to all types of animals in need – protecting domesticated animals like pets and livestock from cruelty, rescuing animals in the wake of disasters, and protecting species from commercial exploitation, habitat loss, poaching, and other threats to the continued health of the population. It has specific efforts devoted to elephant conservation.

TRAFFIC, the wildlife trade monitoring network is a conservation organization born out of World Wildlife Fund and the World Conservation Union and works closely with CITES. TRAFFIC reports on wildlife trade and trafficking and has dedicated much of their reporting to elephant conservation.

The American educational TV channel Animal Planet has a page devoted to elephants and also has several short informational videos online from its program *Wild Kingdom*.

Founded in 1888 as a nonprofit scientific and educational institution, National Geographic focuses on geography, archaeology and natural science, and the promotion of environmental and historical conservation, with specific efforts devoted to elephant conservation. National Geographic has pages dedicated to African and Asian elephants.

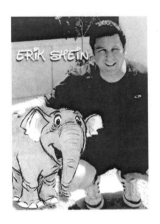

About the Author

Erik Daniel Shein was born Erik Daniel Stoops, November 18th 1966. He is an American writer, and visionary, film producer, screenwriter, voice actor, animator, entrepreneur, entertainer, and philanthropist, pet enthusiast and animal health advocate. He is the author and co-author of over 30 nonfiction and fiction books whose writings include six scientific articles in the field of herpetology. His children's book, "The Forgotten Ornament" is a Christmas classic, and was endorsed by Hollywood legends Mickey and Jan Rooney. Author credits: Animated Film "The Legend of Secret Pass"
https://www.youtube.com/watch?v=SPUJy2DYRZw
http://www.imdb.com/title/tt0765465/combined
http://www.malcolminthemiddle.co.uk/2007/06/20/
frankie-muniz-the-legend-of-secret-pass-movie/

About the Author

L.M. Reker is an educator and author and has written for many years with very diverse groups: gifted, developmental English, humanities, and courses in critical thinking, up to his current position of college professor of English. He has written for an Associated Press newspaper in New Mexico, advertising agencies in Phoenix and LA, has helped write and produce two college texts, and became an assistant chair in the English Department after only one year with that group. He currently collaborates with Mr. Shein on various projects, books, and films.

CPSIA information can be obtained
at www.ICGtesting.com
Printed in the USA
LVOW11s0405040417
529510LV00001B/182/P